THE PASSING OF A PROFIT

AND OTHER FORGOTTEN STORIES

by

H. L. MENCKEN

EDITED BY DOUGLAS OLSON

Forgotten Stories Press
San Francisco
2012

Cover image: Nikol Schattenstein, Portrait of H. L. Mencken, 1927,
oil on canvas, Enoch Pratt Free Library, Baltimore,
reproduced by permission of the H. L. Mencken Estate

Cover design by Kevin I. Slaughter

Published in the United States by
FORGOTTEN STORIES PRESS
P.O. Box 22638
San Francisco, CA 94122
USA
http://forgottenstoriespress.com/

ISBN Numbers:
Hardcover Edition: 978-1-935965-40-4
Paperback Edition: 978-1-935965-41-1
Electronic Edition: 978-1-935965-42-8

First Edition

Library of Congress Cataloging-in-Publication Data

Mencken, H. L. (Henry Louis), 1880-1956.
 The passing of a profit and other forgotten stories / by H. L. Mencken ; edited by Douglas Olson. -- 1st ed.
    p. cm.
Includes bibliographical references and index.
 ISBN 978-1-935965-07-7 (hardcover : alk. paper) -- ISBN 978-1-935965-08-4 (pbk. : alk. paper)
 I. Olson, Douglas, 1954- II. Title.
 PS3525.E43P37 2011
 813'.52--dc23

                2011036612

Contents

FOREWORD

H. L. MENCKEN'S short stories, unfortunately, receive pretty short shrift in the biographies and other reference volumes I have consulted in assembling this collection. Consequently, although it is my belief that I have assembled Mencken's complete output of magazine fiction up to 1906, there is no way to be absolutely sure.

One of the tales retold here, "The Point of the Story," may even constitute a "find," for it appears that it has never been previously attributed to Mencken. It appeared in the "Marginalia" section of *Frank Leslie's Popular Monthly* for September 1901 — the same issue that featured the first appearance of "The Flight of the Victor."

"Marginalia" was a collection of what we would today term short-short stories, sometimes referred to during that era as "storiettes." At that time, it was not unusual for authors to have more than one story in a single publication, with the secondary works appearing either anonymously or under pen names. "The Point of the Story" is bylined "H. L. M.," and, thus, could easily have been overlooked by previous researchers. Mencken would later use that same "H. L. M." signature for more than 200 pieces in the *Baltimore Evening Sun* between 1910 and 1911.

There are other reasons, too, that lead one to consider this a Mencken story. It starts, as do many of the stories herein, with the main character's name. As with others, it uses a newspaper, and newspaper terminology, in developing the situation. And the abrupt ending is in keeping with other stories from this period.

Certainly, none of these similarities, taken by itself, is proof of Mencken's authorship. Nor do all of them, taken together, constitute anything like solid proof. But omitting "The Point of the Story" altogether might deprive the world of a previously unknown Mencken story, so it is included here to keep it from being lost forever. Better safe than sorry!

I wish to thank the Enoch Pratt Free Library, Baltimore, for permission to publish these stories in accordance with the terms of Mr. Mencken's will and his bequest to that library.

Douglas Olson
February 14, 2012

THE DEFEAT OF ALFONSO

DURING THE afternoon of the day that Messrs. George R. Ellicott and James E. Scott, doctors of dental surgery and citizens of the United States, arrived in the city of Cuenca, in the republic of Ecuador, their total monetary receipts amounted to $206 in Mexican silver coin and a one pound note of the Colonial Bank of England.

It had been nearly a year since the last American dentist had visited Cuenca. In the meanwhile, the teeth of the inhabitants thereof had been looked after by a certain Alfonso Iquitos, a gentleman with a forged diploma. As a result, the said teeth were in a sadly dilapidated condition, and, as a second result, the firm of Ellicott & Scott made profits which outstripped the avaricious dreams of the junior partner.

It was an ideal, evenly balanced, smoothly working partnership. Ellicott, the senior member, was a past master in the gentle art of extracting the maximum number of teeth with the minimum amount of pain. His speed record, made in a contest with an English champion at Belize, in British Honduras, was seventy-two in an hour. Scott, the junior, was competent to give expert testimony upon the subjects of crown and bridge work and filling. His views regarding the finer points of the last-named art were undisputed south of the Tropic of Cancer. How the pair had met at the Myrtle Bank Hotel, in Kingston, and signed an agreement to pull together is a story that might be told if it were necessary. But it is not.

Suffice it to say that they arrived at the Cuenca depot, after a tiresome journey across the Spanish Main and over the Andes, with a satchel containing a case of shining instruments, a box of assorted porcelain teeth and six bottles of malleable gold filling. Also, they brought with them a determination to do or die.

When they wrote their names upon the register of the leading Cuenca hotel and hung a huge sign announcing their arrival from the second story window of that hostelry, the emotions of the above-mentioned Alfonso Iquitos were far from pleasant. Whatever feeling of hospitality he may have had toward the newcomers was drowned by the greenest variety of professional jealousy. Their advertisement, upon the editorial page of the daily *Libra*, showed that they were prepared to fill teeth with gold at the rate of $20 Mexican a tooth, and he knew that their operating rooms would be crowded by the elite of Cuenca and the surrounding country. Alfonso himself was never able to obtain more than $12 for the same work. And, besides, he was often compelled to see his patients depart for their homes with their teeth unfilled because of the non-arrival of the gold that he had ordered at Guayaquil or Lima. His credit in the latter towns was not of the best.

Once, in lieu of the king of metals, he had attempted the experiment of filling cavernous molars with an alloy of his own manufacture. Copper and nickel were its chief constituents, and, as he always forgot to inform his patients that it was not gold, he dreamed, for a while, of fabulous profits and a villa in the Andes. But a rascally Americano, the superintendent of a nearby coal mine, dashed his hopes to pieces by exposing the deception.

After that, for several months, Alfonso's lot was a hard one. The people of Cuenca looked upon him with an eye of suspicion, and none but the ignorant peons from the back-woods climbed up his staircase and suffered in his chair. But, gradually, he recovered his lost prestige. His patients began to return to him, for there was no other dentist within two days' journey, and aching teeth, like the tide, wait for no man. And now, just as the sun of prosperity was beginning to shine upon him again, there came Scott and Ellicott, with a blare of trumpets and a flash of red fire, and the winter of his discontent set in anew.

Alfonso was at the depot when the pair of Americanos arrived, and, with true Castilian rage, he watched them enter the finest of all the Cuenca hacks and drive to the hotel. And then he stood beneath the crooked coconut palm in the plaza opposite and saw the people of the town march up, in couples and half-dozens, to have their dental deficiencies remedied. When the sun sank behind the thickets of bananas in the east and the cathedral bell rang the call for vespers, he made his way to his "studio," and there, in the fast-gathering tropical twilight, sat down to battle with his troubles.

For an hour, he remained almost motionless, with his arms folded and his eyes half-closed.

When he arose, the night had come, and the smells of the evening meal were arising from the kitchen of his landlady upon the floor below. And, as he walked downstairs to partake of the repast, he smiled broadly, for a plan to circumvent his rivals was in his brain and the vision of wealth was again before him.

That night, he went to the theater to hear the fair Señorita Attilez sing in *Il Trovatore*, and, after the curtain fell, he went home to bed and pleasant dreams. The woes that had racked him in the morning were gone.

TO EXPLAIN what happened next day, it is necessary to make it known that Alfonso was much like the shoemaker in the fable, whose children caught very bad colds because they were improperly shod. While he had labored upon the teeth of his fellow citizens, he had neglected his own. In consequence, two of his canines, one upon the left side of his upper jaw and one upon the right, were much in need of repairs. A month before, upon a dull day, he had made an effort to fill them, but as his stock of gold was rather low and he found the task a difficult and a painful one, he soon abandoned it. Now there was another dentist in the town, and he would have his teeth attended to. Also, he would look after another little matter that interested him.

Therefore, it came about that when Messrs. Scott and Ellicott arose from their breakfast of fried plantains next morning and entered the waiting room of their apartment, they found the erstwhile leading dentist of Cuenca awaiting them. When he caught sight of them, he arose and made a low bow.

"Eet iss my pleasaire," he said, "to make you a welcome to ze metropaliss."

"Thank you," said Ellicott and Scott, taking his outstretched hands.

"My name," continued their caller, "iss Alfonso de la Iquitos. I am ze gentleman of ze zame profession wis you."

"Ah," said Scott, "a dentist?"

"Si, Señor," replied Alfonso. "I have ze honair."

Then he launched out into a rhapsody upon the science of dentistry, and from that he verged into a highly apocryphal account of his own studies and experiences, and then he gave a history of his residence in Cuenca, and, finally, he touched upon the subject that had brought him to the hotel.

Scott asked a technical question.

"Look at eet," said Alfonso evasively. He took his place in the operating chair and stretched out with his mouth open. Scott examined the damaged canines.

"One of them," he said, "needs filling. The other ought to come out."

"Ah," said Alfonso, "do ze filling fierst."

Then there were polite negotiations, and finally, in consideration of the fact that their patient was a member of the profession, the firm agreed to perform the operation using the best grade of malleable gold for $16 in Mexican silver.

The extraction of the other tooth was to be done *gratis*—as a sort of *lagniappe.*

Scott busied himself with the preparations for his part of the task. Then, when all was in readiness, he set to work with the queer little foot-power drill which had taken the place, in civilized countries, of the ancient rack and wheel. Down into the hard substance of the offending tooth the tiny needlelike point tore its noisy way, and ever and anon Alfonso gasped with pain.

"Does it hurt?" asked Scott, in accordance with the dental ritual.

"Not a mooch," gasped Alfonso, painfully endeavoring to smile. But he stood manfully to his guns, and in time the cavity was ready to be filled.

Then the Americano went to a cabinet by the wall for the filling. As he turned, Alfonso's eyes followed him eagerly. When he opened the drawer, there was a glint of reflected light, and six bottles of the yellow metal stood revealed. Alfonso's eyes fairly bulged from their sockets, and while Scott rubbed up a little glittering ball in the palm of his hand and forced it, grain by grain, into the tooth of the man in the chair, the latter's face wore a smile of surpassing joy.

By and by, after what seemed weeks of agony, the operation was at an end, and Alfonso arose and sought his hat.

"You haf my compliments,'' he said, with a bow. "Eet iss a goot tjob."

"Thank you," said Scott, "the other—"

"Wis approval of you," replied Alfonso, "we vill haf ze pooling—what you say?—*mañana*—tomarrow."

"Make it nine o'clock," said Scott, and, with a second sweeping bow, Alfonso went his way.

From the hotel, he proceeded to his "studio" and arrayed himself in his best frock coat and glossy hat, and for the rest of the day he played dominoes at the club in the Calle Don Pedro. The hours seemed to drag along as slowly as the train which ran from Cuenca to the top of the mountain, and when at last the sun neared the horizon, he arose from the play table with a sigh of relief and returned to his lodgings.

There, he made another change of costume, and an hour later he took his place at the door of the theatre and watched the crowds file in. Senorita Attilez was billed to sing the part of Marguerite in *Faust* that night, and all Cuenca was coming to hear her. Just as the fiddlers in the orchestra began to tune their squeaky instruments, Messrs. Scott and Ellicott crossed the plaza arm in arm and passed through the gaudy entrance. As they brushed by him in the throng, Alfonso bowed to them smilingly, and they asked him, after the manner of their race, how he was. When their forms disappeared through the door which led to the boxes, he turned upon his heel and walked away.

And now comes an unpleasant chapter in the story, for the things that Alfonso did after he left the theatre were not authorized by the laws of Ecuador. First of all, then, he made his way to the little alley which ran behind the hotel. It was as dark and as silent and as deserted as the lowest gallery of an abandoned mine. Then he climbed up to a second-story window, deftly opened the latticed shutter—the windows in Cuenca have no panes—and crawled through. Then he softly tiptoed to the apartment of Messrs. Scott and Ellicott, sought out the cabinet by the wall, pried open its lock with his pocket knife, transferred the six bottles of No. 1 malleable gold to his coat pocket, and departed as stealthily as he had come. Not a soul had seen or heard him. All of the employees of the hotel, except the gentleman who gloried in the title of night clerk, were at the theater, listening to Señorita Attilez. And the gentleman who gloried in the title of night clerk was downstairs in the office, fast asleep.

Straight toward his lodgings Alfonso steered his course.

Once behind their protecting doors, he took the six bottles from his pocket and dumped their contents upon the table. With deft fingers, he rolled the glittering metal into one oblong slab, and with a smile he placed the slab in his inside pocket. The empty bottles he took into the garden behind the house and buried between the landlady's favorite banana tree and the bushy, gaudy croton in the corner. Then he retired to his bedchamber and went to sleep.

Next morning, the prefect of the Cuenca police was hurriedly summoned to the hotel on the plaza. For half an hour, he was closeted with the proprietor and Messrs. Scott and Ellicott. And then the news flew about the town that the Americanos had been robbed. When Alfonso arose and came down to breakfast, his landlady told him the story

"The thieves," she said, "took gold enough to pay a king's ransom."

Alfonso placed his hand upon his breast above his inside pocket.

"Who is suspected?" he asked.

''The bandit Dominiguez,'' said the landlady. "He was seen in the suburbs yesterday morning.''

"Very likely," said Alfonso with a shake of his head.

Then he set out for the hotel. When he arrived, the entrance was crowded by gendarmes and curious idlers. Upstairs, Scott and Ellicott were in conference. The prefect's theory as to the robbers did not appeal to then. They had a theory of their own which seemed to them to be more reasonable. Three years' traveling in South America and the West Indies had taught them a thing or two about Castilian crime.

Alfonso struggled through the crowd and made his way to the Americanos' apartment. He was loud in his condolences. As extravagantly, the victims thanked him for them.

"I had an appointment with you," said Scott, "at nine."

"Ah," replied Alfonso, "I moost release you. Ze unfortune you haf suffaired isst excuse. I am sorrwy. Zis aftairnoon, I moost go away from ze city for ten days. I lament ze unfortune."

"Nonsense," said Scott, with remarkable geniality. "There is no need to cry over spilt milk. The gold is gone, but I don't require gold to extract your tooth."

"Ah, I lament," said Alfonso, but Scott would not hear him, and despite his moving protests and sympathetic tears, he was induced to take a seat in the operating chair and prepare to undergo the ordeal of losing a canine. Ellicott was the extracting partner of the firm, and it was he that opened the instrument case and selected a large, heavy-jawed pair of forceps. Meanwhile, Scott stood by.

With his arms folded across his inside pocket, Alfonso lay back in the chair and opened his mouth. Ellicott examined the damaged masticator with the air of a hangman testing the gallows. Then he opened the jaws of the terrible instrument of extraction and fitted them about it. Then he brought them together upon it with a sudden contraction of the knotty muscles of his mighty right hand, and, at the same time, in violation of all of the rules of scientific dentistry, he sunk the fingers of his left hand into the flesh of Alfonso's neck.

Alfonso jumped like a man struck by a bullet, but Ellicott's fingers did not relax their hold, and he was as helpless as if he were bound and gagged and sewed up in sack. The pain in his tooth was like the torment of a thousand devils, but he could not move. The fingers round his throat made him blue in the face, but he could not move.

Meanwhile, Scott stood by and smiled. "Go through his pockets," said Ellicot after a while. "I've got him dead."

And, slowly, Scott inserted his hand in every pocket in Alfonso's garments. The last one he came to was the inside pocket of the coat. From it, he drew forth the oblong slab of gold. In the light, it glinted brightly. Carefully, he carried it to the cabinet whence it had come and weighed it with a pair of jeweler's scales. It tipped the beam at the exact weight of the gold that had been stolen.

"Is it all there?" asked Ellicott, giving the forceps a little twist. Alfonso trembled like a fever patient and his eyes bulged even further than they had done when he sat in the chair the day before.

"It's all here," replied Scott, and Ellicott released his hold upon his patient's neck and disentangled the sharp jaws of the forceps from the damaged tooth.

Alfonso arose weakly and silently and grabbed his glossy hat. Then he wiped the perspiration from his brow and made a sudden break for the door. And as he dashed out, Ellicott assisted him with the tip of a heavy box calf shoe that bore the imprint of a manufacturer in Jonesville, Connecticut.

The Cook's Victory

"Forced into virtue, thus, by self-defence,
E'en Kings learn justice and benevolence!"
— *An Essay on Man*

CAPTAIN HIRAM JOHNSON, of the oyster pungy *Sally Jones,* thought that buckwheat cakes reached the maximum of deliciousness when they were a light, unbroken brown. Consequently, when Windmill, the colored cook of the *Sally,* placed before him a dozen which ranged in hue from a dirty, speckled russet to a charred and lustrous black, he was very angry indeed.

Pushing his chair back from the swinging table, he leaned against the solitary berth in the *Sally's* cabin and swore earnestly and loudly.

"What do you mean, you black rascal?" he said. "What do you mean, suh, by offerin' me such garbage? Huh?"

"'Deed it war'n't my fault, cap'n," answered his dusky servitor meekly. "Dat dar la'd—"

"Don't you go blamin' it on that la'd!" roared the captain. "Don't you dare do it!"

"I was on'y a-goin' to say—" began Windmill, but the captain refused to hear him.

"I paid ten cents a pound fo' that la'd in Balt'mo'," he shouted, "and you can't find no better nowhere!" He arose and stamped with indignation, "It ain't the la'd; it's you, you shot-faced, black-hearted, gin-soaked—" but the captain's anger paralyzed his tongue, and for a moment he could only splutter and fume. Windmill eyed him with alarm.

"What did I hiah you fo'?" demanded the captain with increased vehemence. "What do I pay you sixteen dolla's a month fo'? To cook vittles or to burn them up?"

As Windmill—who was thus named on account of the unusual prominence of his ears—made no reply to these questions, the captain proceeded to "learn" him, by precept and example, how to fry buckwheat cakes in the manner of the masters of the art. Stalking to the galley, he gave the feeble nut coal fire a few savage thrusts with the poker and began larding the pan. Windmill stood by in silence.

"You take a hunk of la'd as big as a quarter," he said, suiting the action to the word, "and spread it over the bottom of the pan. Then you h'ist a spoonful of battah and dump it onto the la'd—so. You see?"

Windmill replied that he saw, and the captain proceeded to complete the operation. First, he gave the crackling cake a few jabs with the turner, to "loosen it up," as he said, and then, when he thought the under side sufficiently browned, he attempted to turn it. But here he met with difficulties. The cake was fast attached to the pan. Finally, however, after the under side had become a rich black, he succeeded in detaching it, and then, with a deft movement, he slid the turner under it and gave it a graceful toss in the air. It rose as one cake and came down in seventeen pieces.

"Thunderation!" he shouted, turning to the trembling Windmill. "What do you mean, suh, by that, suh?" The cook quailed beneath the weight of profanity which followed.

"You must 'a jogged it too much," he ventured feebly.

The captain's face became a dark, luminous purple.

"Do you mean to criticize me? You black villain!" he asked in a voice which suggested the howl of a storm. "Do you mean to blame it on me when your battah falls to bits?" He shook the pan at the frightened darky's head. "Overboard with it!" he said, seizing the bowl. "Overboard with it!" And he hurled it bodily through the open skylight and spread its contents about the deck above.

The two dredgers who constituted the pungy's crew dodged the flying batter as it came toward them and jumped from the dredge which they had been operating in alarm. On peering down the hatch, they received salutes which cut their investigations short.

The captain, having thus disposed of his breakfast, remembered that he was still hungry, and being in a desperate mood, resolved to cook his meal himself. Windmill, he ordered to stand by for instruction. With infinite pains, he mixed a new bowl of material, and with even greater care prepared the stove and the pan. As he proceeded step by step, he kept up a running fire of sarcastic explanation. At last, the first cake neared completion.

Carefully, he shifted it to the turner and, cautiously, he braced himself to "flip" it. Then he tossed it in the air and it fell intact and right side up—on the stove lid, beside the pan. Windmill jumped to the rescue, and was about to lift it from its resting place, when the broad part of the turner, propelled by the captain's muscled arm, collided with the back of his kinky head, and the captain's heavy shoe-tip came into sudden contact with his "crazy bone." The face of the captain was again a deep, luminous purple.

"Now you've settled your hash for good!" he exclaimed as the cook danced with the pain of the double blow. "Now you can pack your traps and git ashore! Git! You son of unrighteousness! Git! Move! Jump!"

But the cook didn't "git," and neither did he move or jump. Instead, he backed toward the mast and assumed a defensive attitude.

The crew stopped their work and stared dumfounded. Being "shanghaied" men, who had been lured into a shipping office in Baltimore while too drunk to walk unassisted, and placed aboard the *Sally* while in a state of insensibility, they looked with delight upon the threatened war. It might end in their personal gain. But they knew that the captain carried a remarkably fierce-looking pistol in his hip pocket, and when he slowly drew it from its hiding place, they stood at attention, with very respectful expressions upon their unwashed faces.

"Ah!" said the captain with long-drawn emphasis. "Mutiny, is it?" His bushy eyebrows seemed to meet and his beard to stand on end like the fur of a battling tomcat. As he cocked his revolver, the cook grew limp, and slowly and fearfully started to wriggle 'round the mast.

"Ease up!" commanded the captain, and then, to the crew: "Bring up the irons."

The cook halted, and as the captain replaced his revolver in his pocket, began to make a plea for mercy. But the captain was in no mood for compromise. Bringing forth the stump of a cigar from the depths of one of his vest pockets, he lighted it with care, and, after blowing a huge cloud of suffocating smoke from his nostrils, said with solemnity: "You're a dead nigger."

The cook shuddered, and the captain went on: "Yes, you're a goner. You're a mutineer, by Jupiter, a rank, howlin' mutineer. Article two twenty-one, chapter thirteen, verse seven, of the acts of the Legislature of Maryland in Congress assembled covers you all right. 'And if any man shall commit mutiny aboard any vessel in the Ches'peake Bay or tributaries thereof, he shall be taken to the jail from whence he come, and be there hanged by the neck 'till he be dead. And may God have mercy on his soul.' That's the law—chapter and verse."

At this point, the crew reappeared with a pair of ship's irons that had been in the possession of the captain's family since the days when his great grandfather, one Silas Noah Johnson, commanded a Baltimore clipper ship. They weighed little short of fifty pounds and were covered with rust and dirt. Laboriously, the crew pried open the jaws designed to encircle the legs of captives and fitted them about the ankles of the quaking Windmill.

"Lemme go, cap'n," wailed the latter woefully. "I didn't mean no hahm, cap'n. I wasn't a-goin' to hit you."

"By Jupiter, I know you wasn't," replied the captain with fine scorn. "The idear! *You,* hit me! Well, I guess not! But—oh, let it go at that. I think I'll put in at Joneses Point and hang you myself. Hump yourselves, there"—this to the crew, who were painfully trying to lock the irons. "Ain't you got no strength? Shove 'em together!"

The crew, with much difficulty, fastened the irons on Windmill's legs and made the chain fast to the mast. Then they stood by while the captain delivered an harangue on mutiny, hanging and other matters, which fairly bristled with blasphemous metaphors and profane similes.

"Now you get back to work," he said as he ended and went aft. The crew returned to the dredge windlass and soon had it creaking busily. At times, the captain helped them "cull" the oysters which the dredge brought up, and at other times, he labored at the wheel.

Windmill had sunk to the deck, and with the irons encircling his legs, sat disconsolate and silent. That he had done nothing to warrant his execution, he was sure, but he also well knew that on Chesapeake Bay it is customary for each pungy captain to enact his own laws and execute his own sentences. A year before, one Captain Joshua Kellum, under whom he then served, had put him in irons and refused him all food for three days because he had incautiously displayed a revolver. A man whom he had met when last ashore had been locked up in the hold for forty-eight hours because he had questioned his captain's veracity. Memories such as these made Windmill exceedingly downcast.

At intervals, the captain came forward and inspected the irons which bound his prisoner. The latter, more than once, begged to be released. A strong northwest wind had sprung up, and he was becoming numbed by the cold and flying spray. But the captain was obdurate, and to the darky's plaints he made profane and positive answers.

Now, it must not be supposed that he was by nature an unusually cruel or heartless man. As a matter of fact, when compared to the average pungy captain, he was considerate and kind in the extreme. But on this trip, there had been much to vex him.

First, there was the persistent bad luck which had followed the *Sally* since her departure from Baltimore a week before. All the way down the Chesapeake, a series of minor accidents had befallen her. While becalmed off Kent Island, the first night out, the boy whose duty it was to "cull" the oysters taken had escaped by swimming ashore. Then the water cask had sprung a leak, and it had become necessary to secure another at Crisfield. Then one of the crew, by some unknown means, had obtained possession of the captain's whiskey bottle, and by emptying it had become gloriously drunk. Then a sail had been torn and the bowsprit had cracked and a heavy dredge block had fallen on the captain's foot.

Added to these misfortunes was a greater one: The *Sally* had searched in vain for "good ground." On an oyster bed which the captain had discovered on a previous trip, and which he thought that he alone had located, he found a dozen busy "tongers." On the Sells' Point beds were scores of Crisfield boats. Everywhere the *Sally* went, rivals were encountered. This had made the captain exceedingly pessimistic, and in all probability had caused him to recognize signs of mutiny in the cook's inability to fry a perfect buckwheat cake.

At nightfall, one of the crew, by order of the captain, brought Windmill a huge chunk of stale bread and a can of water. The darky, chilled to the bone by the damp bay wind—for it had blown up cold during the day—begged for a release from his bonds, but to all entreaties the captain was deaf. When the latter came forward, before turning in, to light the mast lights, Windmill was in tears, and with much mournful eloquence pleaded for permission to carry his chains below for the night. But the captain still paid no heed to his lamenting.

Before midnight, the thermometer began falling rapidly. Windmill, exposed to the blasts of the storm, shivered and quaked like a fever patient. By crouching in the lee of the water barrel, he succeeded in escaping some of the gusts of cutting wind, but despite his efforts to protect himself, he well-nigh froze. His ears, which many a facetious shipmate had referred to as studding sails, seemed to be dropping from his head, and his arms and legs grew numb. By the time the first faint pink of the dawn showed over the Wicomico shore, he was half senseless.

The captain, in his berth in the stuffy cabin, had rested but indifferently. So far, not more than twenty-five bushels of oysters had been dumped into the *Sally's* hold. The two men of the crew, who had been signed for ten hours' work a day, had labored, on an average, about fourteen. The pungy had been four days on the beds, and she was now far down the bay, within less than fifteen miles of the Virginia line. Of these things the captain thought while he lay awake, and then he thought of the good beds beyond the border. It was true that dredging over there was forbidden to Maryland boats, but, then, did he not know that the sloops of the Virginia oyster navy were unable to be at more than one place at one time, and was it not worth the risk?

Twice before, the captain had attempted poaching. Once he had been successful in eluding the guards, but once the *Sally* had got a shot through her cabin. He debated the matter in detail and at length, and finally decided to try his luck again.

Bright and early next morning, the *Sally* began a slow movement toward the boundary. In the shoal water along the shore, a pretence of dredging was kept up until dusk. While the crew strained and tugged at the windlass, Windmill shivered at the mast. At breakfast time, and again at noon, a slab of bread and a can of water had been placed before him, and he had been commanded to eat and drink. After much begging, he had been given a tarpaulin by the captain, and with this around him, he felt fairly comfortable, though the cold steadily increased.

At sundown, the captain approached him, and in silence unlocked his irons. Then he said:

"You've been reprieved." Windmill stretched his limbs with a sigh of satisfaction. "You've been reprieved," continued the captain, "so as you can help. We're goin' acrost."

With these laconic orders, the *Sally* got under way, and as the moon appeared, she crossed the line and entered the forbidden waters. Windmill was posted in the bow as a lookout, and as the pungy scudded along toward the inshore beds a few miles below the boundary, he craned his neck for a sight of suspicious craft. But he saw none, and soon the crew was hard at work.

Before midnight, the *Sally* drifted into a lot of floating ice. The captain shouted vigorous orders in a hoarse stage whisper, but, by some accident, the vessel became hopelessly entangled, and after an hour's hard labor, the crew gave up in despair, for the ice held her in a strong and unbreakable grip.

Then the captain rose in his wrath and swore from the shoulder deep, comprehensive oaths that made even the hardened blasphemers of the crew stare aghast. The water between the small ice blocks about the pungy was congealing rapidly, and soon there was a straight stretch of ice thick enough to bear a man from the *Sally* to the shore. Fifty yards on the other side was the clear water, and toward this the captain purposed moving the *Sally,* if every man aboard of her was killed in the operation.

With shovels and oyster rakes, the four men attacked the ice, and by dint of much exercise of muscle, began making an appreciable gap in the offshore side. It was killing work, and after an hour of it the crew demanded a half-hour's rest and a "bracer" of brandy. This request the captain answered by striking one of the men in the face with his doubled fist and breaking a rake handle across the other's legs. The crew interpreted these actions as being a declaration of war, and as soon as both had recovered, they made a combined attack on the *Sally's* commander. The jumping and stamping in the conflict which followed made the ice beneath the contestants crackle and tremble ominously, and with mutual accord, they transferred the scene of the battle to the pungy's deck. Here, Windmill went to the rescue of his superior officer, and while he was engaged in "butting" the irate crew with his iron-like skull, the captain had time to dive into the cabin after his revolver.

Waving it threateningly, he sprang on deck. The crew, on catching sight of it, made a simultaneous spring for the ice on the land side, and before the astonished captain had recovered sufficiently to spring after them, they were well on their way to the shore. As he stood speechless on the deck, he heard a voice from the darkness hurl back an avalanche of profanity such as he alone could have surpassed. Then the sound of the deserters' retreating footsteps died out, and the captain turned to Windmill.

"Lord help us," he said piously. "It's five years in the pen."

The cook very sensibly suggested that it would be well to continue their efforts to dig a way to the open water, and the captain silently lifted up a shovel and started to work. Until the dawn, the two labored valiantly. Then the ice began to grow mushy and yielding. Suddenly, it gave way beneath Windmill's feet, and he plunged down into the freezing water.

With much difficulty, the captain dragged him over the side of the *Sally* and carried him into the cabin. The darky was nearly frozen and half scared to death by his sudden bath, and for fifteen minutes lay shivering and speechless beside the stove. When he had recovered sufficiently to go on deck, the ice was breaking up around the *Sally*, and soon it was plain she would be able to pass out into the channel.

Then began work which was to test the captain's seamanship to the full. Slowly and cautiously, the *Sally* made her zig-zag way through the breaking ice toward the open water, completely halted at times by thick pieces, and at other times seemingly on the point of being crushed like an eggshell in the crackling grind. Windmill helped the captain at windlass and rope and wheel until he fairly dropped with exhaustion. His cold hours on deck in chains and his dip into the freezing bay had well-nigh killed him outright, and now, when there was added the fatigue of a night without sleep, it came about that he was in exceedingly unjoyful and rebellious frame of mind.

Just as the *Sally* broke into the channel, a sail appeared to the south, and while the pungy painfully toiled through an acre of drift ice, the vessel, which turned out to be a sloop, gained on her steadily. The captain shaded his eyes to look at the newcomer, and as he did so a puff of smoke spurted from her bow. Then, between the smoke and the *Sally*, the choppy water was lashed as with a whip in half a dozen places, and as he heard a faint, deep "boom," it dawned on him that the sloop was firing on him.

"Lord save us!" he said. "It's the Virginia police boat!"

With his foot, he prodded Windmill. The darky had sunk to the deck and was leaning against the mast.

"H'ist yo'self, you black rascal!" he shouted. "We'll have

to run for it!"

As he spoke, another spurt of smoke spurted from the sloop's bow. Again the water was lashed, and at this time up to a point much nearer the *Sally's* stern than the first time.

The captain, hardly noticing the fact that the cook did not budge, fell to with tremendous energy. Blocks rattled, ropes strained and sails flapped and bellied, and soon the *Sally* was fairly under way. Then, of a sudden and without warning, a lift broke, and the mainsail fluttered to the deck. In a minute, the captain had rudely repaired the parted rope and was straining with all his might and main in an endeavor to hoist the fallen canvas. But the block was rusty and the sail heavy with spray, and despite his gigantic efforts, he could not move it. Meanwhile, the *Sally* drifted and plunged hither and thither, and the sloop came nearer and nearer. At intervals, he heard a "boom" and saw the lashing of the water. Then he bethought him again of Windmill, who still reposed by the mast.

"Here, you enemy of righteousness," he shouted, "h'ist yo'self and lend a hand. Git a-hold of this rope." But Windmill only turned over lazily and said:

"How many years in de pen is it?"

"Five, you rascal," bawled the captain. "Lend a hand at this lift!"

"I think I'll take de five," said Windmill. "It's better dan hangin'!"

The captain's face was a study, as, for the third time, it became a deep, luminous purple. He raised his foot to kick the darky, but just then a shot struck the water not ten yards away, and in consequence, he decided on a hurried compromise.

"Your sentence is commuted," he bawled with much profanity, "to life imprisonment."

But Windmill was unsatisfied.

"Dat's more dan five years?" he said, seeking shelter from the nearing shots on the forward side of the mast.

The captain exploded in a perfect hurricane of wrath.

"I'll make it ten years at hard labor," he yelled.

"Too much," said Windmill.

"Make it seven."

"No, sah."

"Six."

"No."

"Five."

"I'll git dat much hyeh."

The captain began to plead.

"Lend a hand," he said pathetically, "and we'll say a year in jail."

"No, sah," said Windmill, rising. "I hain't goin' to no penitinchry, an' I ain't goin' to no jail. I ain't done nothin' to nobody, an' nobody ain't goin' to hahm me. Dem people ain't goin' to lock me up. I didn't come down hyeh on my own hook. You's de cap'n; not me."

While this long speech was in progress, a shot struck the water so close to the *Sally* that a sheet of spray was dashed over both the captain and the cook. The latter now began to feel fear, and was glad enough to fall to when the captain said:

"Lend a hand, you rascal! You're pardoned!" But first, he demanded a clear understanding.

"No hahm ain't a-comin to me?" he asked.

"No," said the captain. "Now git a-hold of the lift."

"I ain't a-goin' to no jail?"

"No! Git a-hold of the rope!"

"I ain't—"

"Git a-hold of the rope!"

Whereupon Windmill seized the rope, and the mainsail of the *Sally* rose upon the mast, and as a gust of wind bellied it, the pungy shot forward. Then Windmill took the wheel, and the captain prepared to reply to the shots of his pursuers. Bringing from the cabin a rifle of huge caliber and a belt of long cartridges, he took his place behind the wheel and opened fire.

His fourth shot went crashing through the sloop's cabin; his sixth tore a ragged hole through her foresail. The next one struck her mast about ten feet above the deck. A gust of wind gave the timber a timely strain a minute later, and it fell to the starboard, splintered and broken. Then the sloop careened dangerously and came to a stop. The *Sally* was in safety.

THE WOMAN & THE GIRL

GEORGE TIMOTHY GLENK, rebaptized "Whitey" by friend and foe alike, was the possessor of a wild and unkempt head of long, straw-colored hair which might have secured for him immortality as the hero of a Sunday-school novel. In hue, it typified innocence and prayerfulness; in silkiness, it was cherubic; and in length, it was like the wigs of those unfortunate stage children of neuter gender who tearfully stalk through three acts in search of their fugitive fathers.

But Whitey was neither given to tears, to godliness, nor even to cleanliness. He was, in truth, a rather commonplace example of the typical, hard swearing, blasé newsboy, and his chief claim to fame lay in the fact that he was conceded to be the "champeen" buck and wing dancer among his brethren.

His hair hung in a tangled mass over his shoulders because, on the rather rare occasions when he had money enough to have it trimmed, some more attractive means of spending his hoard invariably appeared. A colored friend, a horse-clipper by profession, once offered to perform the operation gratis in order to test a newly-purchased instrument, but this proposal Whitey indignantly and profanely rejected. When his enemies taunted him because of the length of his locks, he silenced them by brute force; when his friends remonstrated, he considered them his enemies.

His years were ten, but to have classed him with the average ten-year-old would have been an injustice. He had the frame of a boy of seven, the profane accomplishments of a stevedore of middle age, and the cunning and agility of an intelligent monkey. In book learning, he was highly uneducated, but of eccentric dancing, he was a master. Constant practice, alone and in competition with rivals, aided by regular visits to theaters of the five- and ten-cent gallery variety, had taught him the technique of the terpsichorean art, and a natural limberness of limb had done the rest. Thus he came to enjoy the sweets of celebrity—merely local, it is true, but still very pleasurable.

There was a belief current among his friends that he had a home somewhere in the city, or that there was a house, or room, at least, whose door stood ajar for his coming and whose inhabitants would receive him as one of them. If he had chosen to satisfy speculation, he might have told of a place in an alley, up three flights of rickety stairs, where there reigned as absolute monarch the woman who had borne him, and in whose presence he stood in awful fear. Sometimes he met her on the street, and, in response to her demand, emptied his pockets of whatever small change they might happen to contain. Usually, however, he kept a wary eye open for her approach, and when she came within his field of vision, took to his heels.

But of such matters he never spoke, and no one had ever seen him in the vicinity of the alley. He had not been there, in fact, since a memorable day, which seemed far in the past, when she was carried off to serve the law because of her victory in a neighborly battle, and he, alone but not helpless, became master of his own destiny. He was then only seven, but by the experience of other boys, he knew that if the law heard of him, he would be doomed to imprisonment in the name of charity. So he sallied forth into the streets and became of the world, worldly.

In summer, he slept beneath steps or in boxes or barrels; in winter, the practice of the graceful art procured for him a welcome from janitors and watchmen who could offer the comfort of a bunk beside a radiator. His food and raiment he obtained in those mysterious ways known only to the genuine gamin. The profits of his paper-selling usually left him by way of a crap game. When his dancing brought forth the gift of a quarter or half dollar from some interested spectator, he would spend it splendidly in treating the gang to a "square feed." But he was seldom given a chance to display his liberality in this manner.

Thus he lived and had his being, and, gradually and almost imperceptibly, there rose up in his soul an Ambition. Slowly, it developed and grew until it became the leading component of his existence, drowning all other emotions and desires, and making him its slave. He yearned to become an actor.

From the choicest seat in the gallery, obtained by standing in line outside the theater entrance from six o'clock until half-past seven, he reveled in the delights of the drama and built those air-castles which histrionic aspirants, male and female, will inhabit until the end of time. Day after day, he studied the posters upon the billboards and dead walls, and, at night, his sleep was made pleasant by lurid dreams, in which he saw himself in the focus of the lime-light, with a full house of applauding spectators before him. When he awoke to the cold realities of an aching back and an empty stomach, the recollection of his visions caused him to forget the absence of pillows and daily bread. Hope made him happy and content and patient.

And, in the course of time, without warning, his day of opportunity came, as it is said to come to all men, great and small.

No Trust Lodge of the Bartenders' Protective and Beneficial Association gave a "full-dress picnic, beer drink and barbecue," and among the "talent" engaged to entertain the members and their "lady friends" were Whitey and a real live actor, the well-known Dutch dialect comedian of the Two A.M. Burlesque Company. This eminent artist had been secured for the occasion by the president of No Trust Lodge, who presided during business hours at the bar of the theater wherein the Two A.M. Company was playing.

He was the lion of the day, and when he applauded vigorously at the conclusion of Whitey's "turn," the latter's happiness was great beyond all imagining. To receive the approbation of such a master was joy and bliss, but to hold converse with him, as was Whitey's lot immediately after, was ecstasy.

"Me boy," said the great man, "you done first rate. I don't rec'lect ever seein' no better." He grasped the blushing dancer's hand and patronizingly patted his head. "Who learned you?" he asked.

Whitey told of his training, and lack of training, and then, becoming more at ease in the presence of greatness, touched upon his Ambition, and, in trembling, watched for the effect his words might have.

"I tell you what you do," said the actor, "you come down to the theater tomorrow night. When the show's over, come around to the stage door and ask for me. I'll take you in to see Smith—Smith's the manager—R. Delano Smith. I guess you seen his name on the paper. Maybe he might be able to use you on the road."

The suddenness of it all made Whitey lose the power of speech, and he left without a word of goodbye or thanks. His brain could formulate no rational thought, and ideas rushed through it in an absurd and eccentric whirl. That night he knew no sleep, for each time his eyes closed in weariness, there came before him a gaudy, dazzling picture as intoxicating and bewildering as a glimpse of the Gates Ajar. In the forefront and center of the dream canvas stood he, himself. Around him, in fantastic throngs, were stage angels, stages Venuses, stage houris, burlesque queens, soubrettes, Irish, Hebrew, German and Negro comedians, stage tramps and musical comedians, and all the other grotesque and varied *dramatis personae* of the vaudeville billboard. Whitey was drunk with joy—maudlin, sodden drunk.

The fact that he had not yet even seen the manager of the show was no damper on his happiness. Had not the leading comedian said that his dancing was well done? Was not that enough? In Whitey, it will be observed, the faculty of logical reasoning was not abnormally developed.

WHEN THE morning came, he appeared in the haunts of his brethren and received their homage. At first, they were disposed to make light of his story, but after he had convinced two or three of the most skeptical by force of physical argument, his claims were acknowledged and all paid him reverence.

When night approached, impatience made the minutes seem hours, and the hours, days. His mind had been too much occupied to allow of his engaging in paper-selling during the day, and, in consequence, he found that his total assets were less than twenty-five cents. With this money, he invested in a "shine" and a five-cent bath. He also visited a cheap barber shop and had his long locks combed, curled and perfumed.

Even then, his clothes made him but a poor imitation of Beau Brummel, and it was with a full appreciation of his sartorial shortcomings that he presented himself at the stage door in the alley behind the theater and asked for "Mr. Smith." The old man upon the older bench within the sacred portal was an awe-inspiring St. Peter, who, from long familiarity with stage-struck unfortunates and other cranks, had learned to be suspicious of all callers.

"What d' you want?" he demanded in a voice which made Whitey quail.

"I come," said the latter, humbly, "to see Mister Smit'. Mr. Levitt told me to be around about this time. He said—"

"Never mind what he said. Didn't he give you his card or sumthin?"

"No sir," replied the boy meekly. This chilly reception

was causing his heart to sink with apprehension.

"Well, then, you don't get in," declared the old man. "Bluffs like your'n don't go around here, lemme tell you."

"But he told me to come," insisted Whitey—and his tone was pleading. "He told me to come. I want to see him. Call him, and he'll tell you."

The old man eyed the boy keenly for a moment and then smiled.

"Aw, come in, then," he said.

Whereupon Whitey went in, and, as if in recompense for his delay at the start, found no difficulty in his path thereafter. In less than a quarter of an hour, he had "seen" Smith and given an example of his dancing. In less than half, he had been engaged and was being measured for a costume. In an hour, he had made the acquaintance of his fellows and was beginning to feel at home. Smith, he immediately observed, was a man little given to unnecessary formality.

The company of which Whitey was to be a member was in course of rehearsal for "the road," and in order to make it deserve, in a slight degree, at least, the encomiums of the bills, Smith was unsparing in his criticism of the various "acts" which made up the "olio." Soubrettes pouted, comedians sulked, and musical artists stormed in secret, but all, it was apparent, held him in fear—as was right. He, alone, they well understood, controlled the perambulations of the "man in white."

Whitey was charmed with his glimpse of life behind the curtain. In a few days, the mechanism of the drama was made plain to him and he became acquainted, aye, even intimate, with the man who produced thunder and lightning. The electrician employed him to polish the brass work of the switchboard and the scene painter permuted him to wash brushes. Once, with the stage carpenter, he climbed high up among the network of ropes above the stage and helped rig the trapeze of the acrobatic team. These were all new experiences, and they gave rise to new and pleasurable emotions. Under Smith's guidance, he spent two or three hours each day in rehearsing.

When the salary question was broached by the manager, Whitey's inherent craftiness caused him to wrangle and bargain, but when Smith heard from his new star's own lips that there was no parent Glenk, he took courage, suspecting no lie, and succeeded in naming a figure eminently satisfactory to himself. Whitey, at the start, was thus, to a certain extent, disillusioned, for it had been his firm belief, as it was of all of his former fellows, that actors' incomes approximate those of the Vanderbilts. However, his weekly stipend included three meals a day, a comfortable bed, and the possibility of buying a new necktie whenever the notion seized him. So he was content.

Slowly, the day before the "first night" approached, and the efforts of Smith to make the initial performance a success were untiring. The last day was spent in a ceaseless rehearsal, but excitement and anxiety drove away fatigue, and when, finally, the orchestra had played the last note of the overture and the curtain rose upon the "opening burlesque," no one of the two dozen eager performers before and behind the backdrop felt too tired to do his or her best. "Turn" after "turn" dragged by, and, one after another, soubrettes and comedians re-entered and re-entered in response to applause and whistles, until Whitey, the supreme moment of his life at hand, stood expectant in the wings.

With a crash, the first notes of a ragtime melody broke in upon the thunder of hand-clapping, and he bounded forth toward the center of the stage. Then his eyes grew misty and he saw nothing but a great, glimmering void. Faintly, as if far away, he heard the music. Before he realized what had happened, he was in the wings again and a loud roar of applause deafened him. Once more he bounded to the footlights; once more he returned, and again the applause, the noise. Five times he thus answered to the call of the gallery gods, and when, at last, he sank into a chair in the dark region behind the canvas trees, his head went round and round and his eyes saw nothing. Then, with a shock, he felt a man's hand grasp his own, and Smith stood before him, smiling and exultant.

"Me boy," shouted the manager in a hoarse stage whisper, "you done great! You done noble! You're all right!"

Whitey was forcibly aroused to a comprehension of Smith's speech by the latter's enthusiastic handshaking. With trembling joy, he hastened to his dressing room. Feverishly, he struggled out of his costume and into the attire of everyday, and then, slowly, he saw the meaning of it all. He was happy, as was his right. For he was a success. He had made a "hit."

During the remainder of the week in town, Smith carefully guarded Whitey from interviews with other promoters of the drama, and by means of well-timed "roasts" for minor delinquencies, succeeded in preventing an enlargement of the boy's cranium. Whitey felt more at ease at each successive performance, and when, at last, the show had got well out upon the road, he began to look upon things, as did the manager and his fellow actors, from the viewpoint of comfort and profit. A two-weeks' tour of one-night stands made him appreciate the blessings of a good bed and good meals fully as much as he did in his days upon the street.

Soon he became accustomed to the gloom and glare of the playhouse, and had an opportunity to look around him on the new world into which fortune had cast him. He saw the life of those behind the scenes in all its naked ghastliness and prosaic commonplace, and he knew the pang which comes with the destruction of an ideal. As, face to face, he met the soubrette whose loveliness had enchanted him when he was yet an unsophisticated gallery god, the greasy red of her erstwhile fair complexion sickened him. As man to man, he met the comedian whose wit had once been charming, he knew him for what he was—a hard-working mechanic, given to drink and the display of artificial diamonds. Actors, in the boy's eyes, became men of common flesh and common appetites, and actresses merely women.

But, on the stage or off, there was one member of the Two A.M. Company whose attractiveness never lessened.

She was known to the public as "Eloise, the Infant Phenom," and to those behind the curtain as Lizzie, the daughter of Mr. James Benson, comedian, and Laura, his wife, whose joint act in the roaring sketch "Asleep In a Cable Car" formed the third turn upon the program each evening. Lizzie was nine, one year Whitey's junior, but her costumes were designed with the intention of making her appear at least three years younger. Her act was like that of the usual "child actress," a few sentimental songs about "daddy" and "dolly," sung in a high, strained voice, a ragtime, a cake-walk, a dance, and the strumming of a "dummy" guitar.

As a drawing card, she was a success, and her father, believing genius to be the infinite capacity for taking pains, labored long and wearily in teaching her the dramatic art. While the other members of the company enjoyed their forenoon slumber, Lizzie usually spent the time rehearsing and re-rehearsing under the direction of her father.

The child was naturally fragile, and the strain of travel and overwork soon made her ill. But audiences could not be disappointed, particularly when the contract called for a deduction of two days' salary for every performance missed, and she "done her turn," as her parent boasted, whether her health was good or bad, or her spirits sad or gay.

As the only flower in a weedy field, as the only being in the company with whom he could converse on anything like terms of equality, Lizzie had attracted Whitey's attention during the first days of rehearsal. By the time the show was a week upon the road, he loved her; at the end of a month, he worshiped her.

Now, it is very disagreeable to see the object of one's adoration subjected to profane handling, even when the intention of the blasphemer is above reproach. The heathen does not relish seeing a scientist lock up one of his gods in a museum, though the latter, in doing so, may intend to insure its preservation. As Whitey heard Lizzie plead and beg for a respite when the hour of rehearsal came round, his collar grew tight and his fingers bent inward. Her upturned, tear-filled eyes were maddening. Her sobbing voice made him frantic.

Deep down in his inmost soul, his chivalry and his manliness were calling upon him to act, but of ways and means, he could find none. Once, he thought of buying a pistol which he admired in the show window of a second-hand store, and of making it his ally. But a wholesome fear of the law, imbibed through his intercourse with the police during his newsboy days, warned him to dismiss the idea. Then he determined to boldly approach Benson and call upon him, in the name of justice and humanity, to cease his cruel conduct, but this, he soon decided, would but bring to him the old reward of the busybody. Whitey, like most of his betters, dreaded ridicule more than any other form of torture.

Having no confidant and no friend of his own age and sex with whom he might even discuss the matter, he grew moody and cynical. At every performance, he danced his dances and sang his songs with spirit and success, but applause, being no longer novel, was beginning to pall, and he found less joy in it than his dreams had led him to expect.

Slowly, the season drew to a close, and the homecoming grew near. As the days and weeks dragged by, Lizzie and

Whitey became firmer and better friends. The bliss which was his because of her apparent reciprocation of his affection was sadly marred, however, by the pain of seeing her suffer. But he took consolation from the fact that the end was at hand, and that the summer vacation, with its restful cessation of toil, would soon be the morrow.

The company arrived in town shortly after noon on Monday of the last week, and there was no time to stop for lunch or rest before the matinee performance. Whitey, on his way with the other members of the company from the depot to the theater, rode conspicuously upon the rear platform of a street car, but none of his former companions were in waiting along the route to welcome him. This neglect stung him to the quick. Had they not heard that the Two A.M. Company was to return that day? And did they not know that he was one of its members? Jealousy of his success, he decided, was the cause of their assumed ignorance of his presence, and this thought made him vow a solemn oath to stare unheeding over their shoulders when chance should make his path cross theirs.

At the matinee, he searched the gallery for familiar faces, but none were there to smile upon him. He went through his act mechanically and with little zest, and, at its end, sat glowering in a dark corner of the vast space behind the back drop.

Lizzie's father was engaged in an animated conference with a heavy-voiced man in a dressing room nearby, and Whitey, from his position, involuntarily heard fragments of their conversation. "Can't do it!" he could hear Benson say, "I'd rather let it alone—them figgers is way under mine," and so on. The other man said, again and again: "Summer season," and the words "easy," "better then nothin'," and "top notch." By and by, they seemed to come to some sort of an agreement. Then they came from the dressing room and, near the door, met the Two A.M. Company's manager.

"Say, there, Mr. Smith," said Benson, "shake hands with Mr. Henderson. He's the manager of the Breakers Beach Casino."

After the greeting had been made, Benson proceeded.

"I just signed with him for Eloise for the summer," he said. "I knowed we'd come to terms. High-class resort, you know—everything first class."

"You're both lucky," said Smith. "You're both got cause to be congratulated. Good act—Eloise's. No better amusement place, I think, than Mr. Henderson's. I—er—of course—I hope that this won't lead you to no changes in your plans for next year, Mr. Benson?"

"Oh, no," was the reply, "not in the least. Mr. Henderson's season starts next week and ends the week before we open up in the fall. The time's completely filled. Three performances a day and two on Sunday. Me and the madam'll rest."

The men continued talking, but what he had heard was enough for Whitey. "Three performances a day!" he exclaimed under his breath, "that man ought to run a sweat shop!" He left the place where he had been sitting as a listener and walked toward the wings. The other members of the company were dressing for the after-piece, and Lizzie was near the end of her turn. In a minute, she came skipping through the narrow entrance and, with the putty-like stage smile still on her lips, almost collided with Whitey. The set expression and pallor of his face frightened her.

"What's the matter?" she asked quickly.

"Come here," he said, and for further answer took her by the arm and led her behind the back drop. "Have you heard about it?" he asked.

"About what?"

"Your old man's doin's."

"No, what's he gone and done?" she said, alarmed by recollection of the time he beat her mother and was himself beaten by a stage hand.

"He signed you for the summer!" exclaimed Whitey excitedly. He was hardly able to keep the lump from his throat. "He signed you for the summer," he said again, "three performances a day! He's a beast—a beast! That's what he is!"

Lizzie took no notice of this slander of her parent, for the tears were coming unbidden to her eyes and soon she was crying softly. Her head found rest on Whitey's shoulder.

"I can't do it," she sobbed with her arms around his neck, "I can't do it! It'll kill me! Oh, I'm so tired, Whitey"—she clung to him despairingly—"I'm so tired, so tired!"

Whitey's face grew hot, and his muscles swelled in strain.

"You shan't do it!" he exclaimed. "You shan't do no such work. You can't stand it!"

Then the impotence of the means at hand to help her was borne to his mind and an angry tear, which he manfully tried to repress, trickled down his cheek. But this was only for a moment. In a flash, determination gained the upper hand of doubt and common sense, and a desperate plan was in his brain.

"You come with me," he said authoritatively. "Come along now! He can't do you no trick like this. I'll take care of you!"

He took the frightened girl by the hand and half dragged her out into the street. With childish logic, she saw reason to be happy in her flight, and almost before they had passed through the long passage to the stage door, her tears had vanished.

As they emerged into the hurrying crowd of the sidewalk, the joy of the victor was Whitey's, and he chuckled as he thought of the surprise and rage of Benson when Lizzie's absence should be discovered.

"Won't he be a sick one!" he muttered in glee. "Won't he

carry on, though!"

They ran the half-block to the corner and turned into the greater thoroughfare, when Whitey stopped with a start and the smile faded from his face. His brain seemed to spin and his muscles grew soft and powerless to move him.

Coming through the crowd, and only a few feet from him, was a figure which he had not seen for nearly a year, but which, in its minutest details, he remembered. A tall, thin woman, with torn and dirty frock, tangled hair, and scarred face, came toward him. When she spied him, she stopped and fixed him in his glare, as a snake is said to paralyze a sparrow. It was the woman who had borne him.

His hold on Lizzie's hand relaxed, and he stood mute and frozen with fear. Neither said a word, but the woman made a step nearer him and raised her outstretched hand as if to seize him. And then he forgot everything in his terror; forgot Lizzie, forgot his courage, his manliness, and his sacred honor, and without a word, dived into the crowd and was gone.

And Lizzie, being of the weaker sex, wept.

The Crime of McSwane

McSWANE LOST his rifle in crossing a river that was not marked upon the map, and the lieutenant pointed out to him, in eloquent language, the evil of the crime of losing it.

"Five minutes ago," he said, "you were a soldier—though a bad one. Now you're a slew-faced, jabbering camp-follower, and useless."

"I couldn't help it, sir," said McSwane. "The log hit me and I went over. The current's faster—"

"To the deuce with the current!" said the lieutenant. "You ought to have held on. Now you can fall out and march with the bearers—and see to it that you don't lose your shirt."

At this, the remaining members of A Company—there were forty-nine—laughed despite their wet rags and thistle scratches, and the captain, who came up at the moment, inquired the reason for McSwane's appearance without his Lee-Metford.

"He dropped it in crossing," said the lieutenant. "I've ordered him to march with the bearers."

The captain nodded in approval.

"Let him keep an eye on them," he said, "until—" The captain turned away.

"Until when, sir?" said the lieutenant.

"Well, until he gets another rifle," said the captain. "He won't have to wait long."

"No, it won't be long," assented the lieutenant. And so McSwane marched over to the place where the black bearers of burdens were jabbering, and watched the black boss bearers count them and beat them into line. His fellow warriors of A Company laughed as he moved away, for it was funny to see a private in a British regiment of the line reduced to the level of a Hausa draft animal, and in the jungle, the minor refinements and kindnesses of life are forgotten—particularly by gentlemen who knew little of them at home. It was cruel, perhaps, to laugh at McSwane, for his misfortune was the result of an accident, and he was not to blame, and most of the others would have wanted to fight—as he did now—if he had laughed at them, but, nevertheless, it was the best joke they had heard since the day they landed at the coast, and so they laughed and were merry.

Few things of an amusing nature, in truth, had happened to the men of A Company for many a day. Summoned from Lagos to help keep the Queen's peace, they were now on their way through the jungle and the tropical forest to a certain town up-country, which had an unpronounceable name beginning with N'B and a heathen king who had indulged some time before in the luxury of leisurely and artistically massacring a Presbyterian missionary and a dozen or two native converts. It would be the duty and pleasure of A Company to discover and surround, and later to capture and hang this monarch, and to kill as many of his soldiers as might come into rifle range and to burn as many of his villages as might appear, and so the men marched uncomplainingly through the sodden grasses and lay awake nights with chills and staggered along during the day beneath a big red sun that almost set their helmets afire.

In the lead marched the first lieutenant, with half of the men and the machine gun, and then came the black bearers, with boxes of cartridges and canned beef and hard crackers and quinine, and after them, the captain, in a hammock borne by four blacks, and then, last of all, the rest of the men, with the sick plodding along as best they could among them.

McSwane now marched in the rear of the last bearer—they were stumbling along the narrow jungle path in single file—and a few yards ahead of the first man of the rear guard. This first man, who had a reputation as a wit, was determined to relieve the pain and tedium of the journey by making McSwane entertain him. Accordingly, he invented a number of humorous remarks about soldiers without guns and white bearer bosses and clumsy rookies, and voiced them in a tone calculated to allow those behind him to hear them and enjoy them. The latter, after each effort, passed the witticism along, and a wave of laughter traveled down the line to the last man dragging in the rear.

For half a day, McSwane listened to all of this in silence, for a source of consolation was open to him of which his taunters seemed to be unaware. But, finally, the great red glare of the sun or something else prompted him to make a strike for peace, and he turned around and smiled grimly.

"Was you there when the captain come up?" he asked.

"That I was," answered the wit, "an' I heerd him call yer a slew-faced, jabberin' camp follower."

"No," said McSwane calmly. "The captain didn't say that; it was the lieutenant."

"Well, what did the captain say, then?" asked the wit, parrying for an opening.

"The captain sez," replied McSwane, "'Wait 'till he gits another rifle. *It won't be long!*"

"Well?" said the wit, more soberly.

"He meant that one of you wooden-headed clodhoppers is goin' to get a bullet through your little gizzard before long, and that I'll git the dead man's gun." McSwane paused a moment. "And, by God," he continued fiercely, "*I hope that man'll be you!*"

There was a gradual cessation of laughter all along the line, and the wit tripped over a vine, and in stopping to swear at it, allowed a score of other men to pass him. McSwane turned to the new leader of the rear guard and glanced at his rifle.

"You heerd what the captain said?" he demanded.

"Yes, I heerd it," replied the man, shuddering, and McSwane plodded on again in peace.

That night, when A Company and the bearers halted in a clearing to eat and sleep, men of the rear guard told those who had been in the van of the dialogue between McSwane and the wit. Most of the men had heard the colloquy between the captain and the lieutenant, but few of them had thought of the real meaning of the captain's words. Now, however, they saw it all very clearly, and it did not make them very comfortable.

McSwane came over to the mess with his fellows, and they dealt him his share of canned beef and hard crackers and allowed him to fill his canteen. But few of them spoke a word to him, and all of them seemed bent upon keeping out of his range of vision. At times, before the dark closed in, he roamed about the camp and stared sullenly at the men. Whenever his gaze fell upon a rifle, its possessor turned pale and felt nervous and ill at ease.

As the sun went down, a black runner came into camp and the officers and interpreter took him to one side and questioned him. Before long, as news filters down the ranks in a regiment or a company, the word was passed along that the runner was a spy and that he had reported that the blacks had built a big stockade across the road five miles ahead. This stockade, according to the report in its final form, was by far the largest and most formidable in all Africa. McSwane sat on a fallen log at the edge of the camp and listened as half a dozen of the men discussed it.

Just as one of them was drawing, with great attention to detail, a picture of its strength, he rose, knocked the ashes out of his pipe, and turned to walk away.

"There," he said, "is were I git my rifle."

And he laughed a laugh that made the others so uncomfortable that the discussion of the stockade ceased.

NEXT MORNING, the company was on the march before sunrise, and by the time the purple light of the morning began to filter down through the palms, the captain had pushed on ahead and the column was moving slowly and very cautiously through the forest. Five men and the lieutenant—serving as the "point"—marched a quarter of a mile ahead of the others, and ten more men struggled along through the undergrowth to either side of the path. In the van of the column proper were forty Tommies and the captain, and then came the black bearers, with McSwane leading them. The bearers, scenting danger, and knowing from the slow pace of the column and the frequent halts that it must be near, were disposed to fall ill by the path side and to be lamed by all sorts of thistles and brambles, and to be bitten by various invisible scorpions and snakes. McSwane turned upon them now and then and calmly belabored them with a bamboo club, and they shrieked and jabbered and stumbled on again.

Suddenly, from afar, came a loud, heavy rattle, like that of a steam crusher breaking stone. In a moment, it rose to a shrill roar and then it continued, in fits and starts, now loud, now not so loud, now ceasing altogether. The Tommies smiled as they heard it; it was the machine gun clearing the way, and they knew that the battle was on.

Soon, the men in front of McSwane started ahead at the double, and the captain shouted loud orders to them. In a moment, there was a widening clear space in the pathway before McSwane, and then, to the consternation of the bearers, the rear guard came dashing up and over them and on ahead in the track of the van. The men were out of breath and perspiring, and as they passed McSwane, a good many of them seemed badly scared. Before he could frame a sarcastic remark to fling at them, however, they were gone.

For a few moments, he trudged on in silence. Ahead, the

rattle of the machine gun was growing louder, and soon the sharp crack of the Lee-Metfords mingled with its sound, and all of the weird noises of a battle rose into a dull, uneven banging. Plainly, thought McSwane, it was a battle worth seeing and here he—but why?—was the rear the place for a soldier? Was the head of the bearer train the post of a fighting man?

Of a sudden, he sprang forward and ran, at the top of his speed, toward the fight. Up the narrowing path he ran, around two sharp turns and then into the open. Far ahead, half hid in the undergrowth, was a palisade of heavy logs, and from it came spurts of flame from trade guns. Before it, in the grass, lay the men of A Company, firing at the palisade, the spurts of flame and the black faces that peered above.

To the right, the machine gun was squirting fire at the flank of the fortress, and to the left, ten men and the lieutenant were fixing bayonets for a charge.

McSwane grasped the entire scene as if it were painted on canvas, and then he dashed on and a stray bullet from a trade gun came whistling by and tore the crown from his helmet. McSwane laughed—and tripped over something in the high grass, and went sprawling. The something was Murphy of A Company, with a bullet in his leg, and McSwane stopped short and reached for Murphy's rifle.

"Go 'way!" shrieked Murphy. "Go 'way, you grave-robber!"

"Gimme the gun!" exclaimed McSwane.

Murphy swung the rifle 'round and pointed the muzzle at McSwane's head.

"Go 'way!" he cried. "Go 'way!"

McSwane turned and ran on, and a few seconds brought him to the line of men in the grass.

"Lie down, you ass!" shouted the captain.

McSwane stared ahead foolishly for a moment, and a

swirl of bullets from the trade guns whistled all about him. Then he dropped to all fours and crawled across the line, stopping a moment at the side of each man.

"I want a gun!" he wailed crazily. "I want that gun I was to git!"

"Go 'way, you beast!" exclaimed one of the men. The whole line shuddered at sight of him, and as he came to each man, each drew away from him as if he were a plague patient.

"I want that gun!" he wailed. "Where's my gun?"

Suddenly, the bugle sounded, and the men crouched as if for a spring. Then there was another note and they scrambled to their feet and ran ahead, to charge the stockade from the front and to capture it or die. McSwane sprang to his feet with them and rushed thither and hither among them before they began the charge. When they got under way, he rushed on ahead of them, over the tangled grass and the fallen tree trunks, and toward the great log fortification and the trade guns. Twice he fell and once another man fell over him. The other man sprang aside in terror.

"Go 'way!" he shouted.

In a moment, the men reached the stockade and the captain scrambled up the face of it. McSwane leaped against the rough logs beside him.

"Here's where I git that gun!" he shouted jubilantly. "Here's where I git my gun!"

A volley from the trade guns and a volley from the Lee-Metfords poured forth at the same instant, and McSwane fell from the face of the stockade and writhed upon the ground. There was a small, clean-cut hole in his neck, where a bullet had torn its way into his flesh and his life.

And—though this never appeared officially—it was not a bullet from a trade gun that made it.

Like a Thief in the Night

NECESSITY, THE mother of invention, led Messrs. Brown and Tankersley to organize the Lyricio Opera Company. For months, the lesser Antilles had treated them with little kindness. Trinidad had rejected them as journeyman dentists. Grenada had frowned upon their efforts to establish a newspaper. St. Lucia had egged them from the patent medicine rostrum and dumped their store of headache pellets into the sea. And now they were in St. Pierre, Martinique, with ten pounds sterling in ready money and a pair of empty trunks.

Perhaps it was mere chance that caused M. de Bourges to fall from grace upon the day of their arrival. Messrs. Brown and Tankersley thought that it was Providence. At any rate, it was good luck, for it blazed the way for the longest spell of prosperity they had enjoyed since the wrecking of the steamer *Tomaso*.

M. de Bourges, it should be known, was an impresario. Provincial France having applauded him, he sought to dazzle Paris. But Paris is too old to be dazzled, and, in consequence, he failed. Then he bethought him of the colonies—the simple-minded, good-hearted colonies along the Spanish Main.

A month after this thought struck him, he landed at St. Pierre, with a huge pile of scenery and "props," and a score of seasick singers. Mlle. Avignon, "the peerless soprano dramatique," was in the party. She was the prima donna. And then there were M. Declasse, the tenor robusto; and Mme. Le Brun, the contralto; and the Señor Badajoz, the basso; and the members of the "giant" chorus.

All Martinique attended the first performance; the receipts were three thousand francs. Mlle. Avignon was charming, and M. de Bourges was charmed.

"Ten nights like this," said he, as the final curtain fell, "and I'll pay all expenses. Twenty—and I'm a rich man!"

But the people of Martinique apparently thought one night at the opera enough for a single year, for, by the end of the first week, the audiences had dwindled to a mere handful. On the eighth night, the cash receipts were a hundred and thirty-four francs.

Next morning, before dawn, the steamer *Giaour* came in from St. Lucia, with Messrs. Brown and Tankersley. When she pulled out, as the sun rose, for the north Atlantic and France, M. de Bourges sat meditating in the shade of her funnel. His woes had been too many for him. He was homeward bound to escape them—and the score of singers behind him awoke to find themselves stranded.

Then appeared Messrs. Brown and Tankersley—first in the role of ready sympathizers.

"Meesraable rescaal!" shouted the Señor Badajoz.

"Veelain!" cried Mme. Le Brun.

"A shame!" said Messrs. Brown and Tankersley.

Thus the negotiations began. For two days and two nights, in the parlor of the Versailles Hotel, they continued. At first there were many halts, for the Señor Badajoz was suspicious of all impressarii, American or otherwise. Then there were other halts, for the *Americanos* distrusted the Señor Badajoz. Finally, however, a neutral ground was reached and the bond was signed and sealed. As the last autograph was blotted, the terms were recapitulated.

"Mr. Brown and myself," said Tankersley, "agree to act as managers and booking agents. We will be responsible for all coin hauled in and paid out. You, John R. Bad—"

"Juan," corrected the Señor Badajoz.

"You, John R. Badajoz," continued Tankersley, "agent for the rest of the company, agree to put up the scenery—seized for unpaid salaries from M. de Bourges, skipped—and to pay your way to Kingston, Jamaica. There, we agree to take you in charge and put up all future coin—your salaries to be the same as under M. de Bourges. Am I right?"

"You air right," said the Señor Badajoz.

"In witness whereof," said Tankersley, "we have hereunto set our hands and caused our great seals to be placed."

"Done," said Brown.

TWO DAYS later, the reconstructed company set sail in the tramp steamer *Yucatan*. While she beat about in a half-hearted hurricane and the score of artists groaned in their staterooms, Messrs. Brown and Tankersley considered ways and means. First of all, they decided upon a name for their organization.

"Call it the Lyricio Opera Company," suggested Tankersley. "It sounds foreign-like—Spanish, maybe."

"It's poor Spanish," said Brown.

"Well, then," replied Tankersley, "we'll say that it's Choctaw."

And so the company was named.

Next followed the consideration of a route. Kingston was chosen as the point of beginning—then Port Antonio, Montego Bay, Kingston again, Belize, in British Honduras, and the isthmus. Ten hours were spent in an argument as to the advisability of stopping at Colon. Colon has been long known as a good "show town," but there was a chief of police among its officials who did not like Messrs. Brown and Tankersley. It was the middle of the third day out when they finally decided to "cut" it. An hour afterward, the *Yucatan* was fast to the dock behind the Myrtle Bank Hotel, in Kingston.

It might be interesting to tell how the company made a hit and much money in the Jamaican capital, and a bigger hit and less money at Port Antonio, but all of this would be beside the point, for the real scene of this story is Montego Bay, a funny little town in the far northwestern corner of the island. The first causes, however, sprang into being some time before the singers reached the bay. They had their rise in the peculiar temperament of the Señor Badajoz.

When the *Kingston Gleaner* said that his voice was "the greatest ever lifted in song south of the tropic of Cancer," he demanded a fifty-percent increase in salary. When the officer commanding Her Majesty's forces at the Up Park Camp invited him to sing "Rule Britannia" at a reception, to the officer administering the government, he requested that the other warblers in the company address him as "excellencia."

To both of these demands, Messrs. Brown and Tankersley made curt refusals. Thereupon, the Señor Badajoz grew sulky and for three days declined to hold any converse whatever with his employers. Not until pay day—the day that the ghost walked—did he seem to be aware of their existence. Then he remarked that they were money-grubbing savages and ex-herders of swine.

This slander was highly distasteful to Messrs. Brown and Tankersley, and in their hotel room that night, they discussed the means of vengeance.

"We must fire him," said Tankersley.

"On the spot," added Brown.

"We can't," said Tankersley, fumbling in his pockets. "The contract says—" and he spread the paper upon the bed—"See here—"

As Tankersley's finger followed the lines, Brown read aloud: "'When the said parties of the first part'—us," explained Tankersley, "'wish to dispense with the services of one of the parties of the second part, they must give notice before the first of the month, and the said dispensing shall take effect on the first of the month. If notice is not given before the first, the said party of the second part shall not go until the first of the next succeeding month.'"

"Do you see the point?" said Tankersley.

"We'll be in Montego on the first," replied Brown. "From the thirty-first to the second. Today's the fifteenth. We'll give him notice tonight."

"Foolish!" said Tankersley. "He'd bust up the show."

This view, on second thought, also appealed to Brown, and after some further discussion it was resolved that the Señor Badajoz was to be given "his notice" after the performance upon the night of the thirty-first, at some time between the fall of the curtain and twelve o'clock midnight.

Now, the night of the thirty-first was scheduled to be the night of the Lyricio Company's debut at Montego Bay, and as the schedule provided, so it came to pass. Artists and managers arose before the sun that morning, and when the little two-coach train pulled out of the depot in the dim light of the tropical dawn, they sleepily attacked the breakfast of mangoes and goat sandwiches provided by the inky train boy. For five hours they rode, northward and westward, up the steep slope of the Nassau Mountains and down the other side. At times they were flying through dense thickets of bamboo and bananas; at other times they were on the crest of some heaven-kissing hill, and the green and gold of the sparkling Caribbean lay far below them. It was like a journey into fairyland—but the Señor Badajoz did not note its charms.

This was because he had received a premonition of his fate. Mlle. Avignon, with a woman's power of divination, had guessed the plans of Messrs. Brown and Tankersley, and though she did not like the Señor Badajoz, the tie of fellow craftsmanship had prompted her to warn him.

"Swine herders!" exclaimed the Señor with heroic wrath.

"You must outwit them," said the sympathetic mademoiselle.

"Ah!" replied the Señor Badajoz gloomily, "I must think!" And with his head resting upon his fists, he proceeded to do so, and while thus engaged, he was blind to the earth and the sky and the sea.

The result of his painful cogitation was not shown until the time came, that night, for lowering the final curtain. The performance had been a success. The Señor had never been in better voice. True enough, there was an air of preoccupation to be noted in his acting. Twice he tripped over his stage sword. Three times he stepped upon Mlle. Avignon's train. But the people of Montego Bay ascribed these lapses to artistic eccentricity, and, in consequence, applauded all the more.

Messrs. Brown and Tankersley stood in the wings. "We must get him before twelve," said Tankersley.

"Or we'll have him for another month," said Brown.

"I must hide until after twelve," said the Señor under his breath, as he launched into the grand finale.

At half past eleven, to the second, the bell rang for the final curtain. As it came lumbering down with a hitch and a halt, Messrs. Brown and Tankersley stepped to the door of the Señor's dressing room. And at the same moment, the Señor glided through the wings at the other side of the stage and climbed out of a window. As he dropped into the darkness, he laughed aloud. It was a mocking laugh, and Messrs. Brown and Tankersley heard it. And as they were gentlemen well schooled in wit and craft, they solved its meaning before its echo died away.

"Skipped!" exclaimed Tankersley.

"Skipped!" exclaimed Brown.

In a second, Tankersley had shed his coat and grabbed a coil of rope which hung pendant from the flies. In another second, he and Brown were in the street. A hundred yards away, they caught sight of the Señor. He was galloping toward the outskirts upon a mule. And as he heard them yell, he laughed again.

It was a mocking laugh, and very unfortunate for a certain gentleman of color. This gentleman, at the moment, was passing the fruit warehouse "theatre" with a team of mules.

He had halted his cart to stare at the flying Señor and the crowds and the lights, and was altogether unprepared to be attacked by highwaymen.

But Messrs. Brown and Tankersley were not accustomed to saying "by your leave," and then and there, in the presence of the beauty and fashion and chivalry of Montego Bay, they set upon the said gentleman and wrested his team from him. And then, before the astonished spectators could utter a sound or raise a hand, they tore the mules from the cart, sprang to the animals' backs, and set off at a killing gallop up the road.

The chase which ensued will be remembered at Montego until some festive hurricane wipes the town from the map. With one hand, Tankersley clutched the bridle of his steed and with the other he held fast to the coil of rope. And with his voice and both of his heels, he urged his mule to move lively.

Down the main street, the pair of pursuers dashed — past courthouse and lockup, and out of the region of houses and into the open country. As they reached the gate of the first plantation house, they caught sight of Señor Badajoz.

"Halt!" yelled Tankersley.

For reply, the Señor laughed a third time.

"Halt!" yelled Tankersley again, drawing a revolver from his hip pocket. And as the Señor opened his mouth to laugh a fourth time, a bullet kicked up the dust a yard behind him.

Then his hair rose on end, and his laugh died upon his lips, and he turned his galloping mount into a dark little plantation road to the left. In the first ten yards, the animal stumbled twice, but the Señor urged him on and on, for, as he had turned, a second bullet had whistled over him.

The beat of his mule's hoofs upon the soft pathway aroused the furred and feathered denizens of the roadside thicket from their midnight naps. A scared mongoose fled headlong before him, and a lone parrot in a towering bread-fruit tree cawed a frightened protest. Once, a big coconut came tumbling down from its place a hundred feet in the air. But though it narrowly missed breaking his head, the Señor did not heed it, for he was in a hurry.

Suddenly, he came to the end of the road, and his mule, as if by instinct, swerved into a banana field. Down a lane between the ungainly trees the animal leaped and plunged.

The moon was full that night, and on the highway it was as light as day. But, beneath the shadows of the towering bananas, there were spots of inky blackness, and it was in these places that the Señor's mule ran aground. But, by dint of much tugging and yelling, he managed to retain his seat, and when the pair of *Americanos* turned into the lane, he was a good hundred yards ahead of them.

Then began the dash down the home-stretch. The pursuers, more lucky in their mounts than the pursued, floundered along with few falls. In a moment, the distance between them was lowered to eighty yards, and to fifty, and to twenty-five. And as they dashed on, Tankersley dropped his bridle and, with both hands free, made a slip knot in the rope at his side. Then Brown dropped back and Tankersley swung the rope clear above his head.

Suddenly, a stealthy coil of some sort wrapped itself about the Señor and dragged him from his mule. As he struck the soft earth with a heavy jar, it was drawn taut and he lay helpless. And then Messrs. Brown and Tankersley were upon him.

"You are discharged!" yelled Brown.

"We give you notice!" yelled Tankersley.

And as they bent over him, to disentangle him from the snares of their lasso, the tones of a deep-voiced bell came floating upon the night air.

It was the church clock of Montego Bay, and it was striking twelve.

The Flight of the Victor

IN THE beginning of things, the state of journalism in Kingston—from the standpoint of comfort, if not from that of profit—was highly satisfactory to the gentlemen who labored in its ranks. Two dailies there were, the *Times* and the *Herald,* and to both the advertisers of Jamaica extended a fairly liberal patronage. The proprietor of the former was Mr. George Algernon Gorson, the eleventh son of a needy baronet, and, for a brief year, a lieutenant in a British regiment of the line. The proprietor of the latter was Mr. Fitz-James FitzHugh, a native of Ireland and a citizen of the world.

Now, Jamaica, since the discovery of the fact that the banana is a valuable fruit, has been divided, as to politics and population, between the Original English and the Interloping Americans. The English, being in charge of the government, look upon the Yankees as their subjects. The Yankees, having control of the banana plantations, and, in consequence, of three-fourths of the island's lands and nine-tenths of its revenues, regard the Britons as semi-barbarians—too torpid to be enterprising and too ignorant to make money.

Thus it happens that there are two camps in politics, in society and in trade, and thus it happened that of the two newspapers at the beginning of things, one was loyally British and the other was American to the core. The *Times,* as may be supposed, was the government organ. As an ex-officer of Britain's glorious army, Mr. Gorson was a believer in British customs and British traditions. By the same token, the *Herald* was the organ of advanced Americanism. Hating the assertive English with a brotherly hatred, its proprietor bestowed his regard upon the assertive Yankee, and, bravely, he battled for the latter's rights and privileges.

Despite this diagonal opposition, and despite, also, a marked personal enmity, the proprietors of the *Times* and the *Herald* realized that, in some matters, at least, an armed truce is more profitable than perpetual warfare. Britons they were, and, Briton-like, they lacked the overpowering news lust of the American newspaper man. Besides this, they lived in a town where *mañana* is the motto of the multitude. In Kingston, the sun is warmer than in New York, and it is more painful to hustle. Therefore, when the shades of evening fall and the cooling land breeze comes down from the mountains, the sun-dried Kingstonians long to array themselves in comfortable khaki and sip refreshing liquors in the gardens along the sea-wall.

"Let us labor," they say, "when the sun is up and it is too warm to enjoy idleness. When the dark comes, let us rest beneath the palms."

Thus it happened that the staffs of both the *Times* and the *Herald* lay down their pens and shears at an hour when the men who make American morning papers are fairly beginning work. At five o'clock in the afternoon, the black foreman of the *Times* printing department appeared at the door of the editorial room and made a polite but stentorian request that the men at the desks bring their writings to a hurried close. At half-past five, the last batch of copy was cut into takes and distributed among the dark-skinned girl compositors. At seven o'clock, the late page was made up, and at eleven, the *Times'* edition of four thousand paid-up had been run from the lumbering press. And from that time until five o'clock next morning, when the early mail train pulled out for Port Antonio, and the score of carriers began work in Kingston town, the *Times* lay dormant. The post-office telegraph office usually closed at dusk, and after that, except under extraordinary circumstances, no news from beyond the sea came over the wire. If there was a fire, or a murder, or an earthquake, or a massacre in Kingston, the subscribers of the *Times* were willing to wait for the details until the morning of the second day.

By the terms of the unwritten agreement mentioned, the *Herald* staff, in like manner, ceased labor when the sun went down. If one paper had broken faith by waiting for late dispatches, the other, in self-protection, would have been compelled to do likewise. But neither seemed inclined to do so, and, in consequence, the people of Jamaica came to look upon history as news.

This was the state of affairs in island journalism when Mr. Harris Morgan took service with the *Herald.* Mr. Morgan was an American, and for five of his twenty-five years he had labored "on the street" for a New York yellow journal. How he came to surrender his commission and to journey to Jamaica is immaterial. Suffice it to say that he was made sub-editor of the *Herald*—which means everything but editor-in-chief—at a salary of fifty shillings a week. Two months after he began his duties, an accumulation of debts caused Mr. FitzJames FitzHugh, the proprietor, to depart inconspicuously in the steamer *Giaour,* for Liverpool. Thereupon, by the unanimous consent of his late chief's creditors, he was made editor, manager, and practical owner of the *Herald.*

Though it jarred his journalistic sensibilities, Mr. Morgan was not blind to the advantages of the unwritten agreement between the *Herald* and the *Times.* When the evening land-breeze scurried over Kingston, he well appreciated the joy of laying down his labors, and when the dark came with tropical suddenness, and the dull, red sun was gone, he thought it infinitely pleasant to sit in the waterside garden of the Myrtle Bank Hotel and sip a glass of plantation rum and lime juice. Mr. Gorson, of the *Times,* also loved his ease at his inn, and many a time the two sat side by side until the damp chill of midnight drove them indoors and to bed.

Thus it was that a highly satisfactory *entente cordiale* sprang into being. That it might be preserved, Mr. Morgan resisted, six times in two weeks, the temptation of halting the *Herald's* press to make room for a late telegram. It was during the rumor-ridden days before the first gun was fired in Cuba that he was thus tempted, and four times Mr. Gorson was tempted also. Three times, he held fast, but the fourth time, he surrendered, and next morning, the *Times* appeared with a big beat at the top of its column of post-office cablegrams.

Mr. Harris Morgan, the editor of the *Herald,* read the story at breakfast. When he had finished his third mango, he arose from the table, folded his copy of the *Times* into a handy compass, placed it in his pocket and walked calmly along the shady side of Harbour Street to his office. Not until he was seated at his desk did he move a muscle of his face. When he did so, it was to smile and say, "Ah!"

Next morning, the *Herald's* subscribers were given a shock of exceeding surprise. Across the top of the telegram column, instead of the customary and innocuous legends, "England" and "America," there staggered a heavy line of black-faced job type. Below it was a double line of smaller type, and below that a pyramid an inch and a half in height. It was the first scare head ever printed in a Jamaican newspaper, and below it was the first "fake" of any magnitude ever perpetrated upon the Jamaican public.

How the said public regarded the scare head and the fake was at first a matter of doubt. But Mr. Harris Morgan believed that both features would make a hit, and in this, time proved him to have been in the right. "The British," he reasoned, "though slow, are human, and it is one of the failings of humanity to be enthralled by black type and sensational stories." And in accordance with this theory, though Mr. Gorson, of the *Times,* thundered daily against "our vulgar contemporary's exaggerated dispatches," Mr.

Morgan laid on ink with a lavish hand, until the *Herald's* scare heads stretched across three columns, and the texts of the dispatches were set in type half an inch in height. The Britons of Jamaica, after a week or so of pained doubt, rushed to the standard of the *Herald* in an excited body, and in two weeks it had captured fully a half of the *Times's* subscribers. The black type had won, and the winter of Mr. Algernon Gorson's discontent had begun.

Then arose a fierce and decisive battle between American ingenuity and English pounds, shillings, and pence. The *Times,* with long years of prosperity behind it, had money in the bank, and Mr. Algernon Gorson, determined to do or die, drew liberally upon this money to beat his rival. At an expense of fifty guineas a week, an agreement was made with an English news agency whereby half a column of late news was to be cabled to the *Times* each night. At a further expense of two guineas a week, arrangements were made whereby the Kingston post office telegraph clerks remained awake until after midnight, in order that late messages from overseas might be rushed at once to the *Times* office.

Within the confines of the office itself, a wonderful revolution took place. No more did the black foreman of the composing-room call for the last batch of copy before sundown. No more did the editor and proprietor partake of limeade in the garden of the Myrtle Bank Hotel. Until the light was long gone and the dawn of the next day was nearly come, the type clicked and the pens scratched, and the perspiration stood out in beads upon the foreheads of editor, sub-editors, and compositors. Accounts of night fires "got in," and late stories of the day's doings in Kingston were double leaded. As the land-breeze died, the presses began their rumbling, and not until the east was red and gleaming did they cease.

In the office of the *Herald,* there was like bustle and industry. Unable to spend sixty pounds a week for authentic news by the cable, Mr. Harris Morgan labored early and late in manufacturing the unauthentic kind. With copies of the *Times* and the week-old New York papers at his side, he wrote telegram after telegram, and as he was a young man of much ingenuity, with five years' service in a yellow journal office to aid him, he frequently came very near coinciding with the belated truth.

The people of Jamaica, being Britons, would have manifested no interest in the threatened war had it not been that there was great likelihood that it would be fought in the shadow of their homes. Mr. Morgan, noting this fact, gave them liberal doses of the kind of news that they craved. Daily, the *Herald* announced that American cruisers were "hovering off the north coast," and, daily, its "special correspondents" wired intelligence of "heavy firing near Montego Bay" and "suspicious evolutions in the Windward Passage."

And, meanwhile, Mr. Algernon Gorson, racking his brains to discover the source of his adversary's dispatches, gave way to despair. One day, a particularly exciting telegram in the *Herald* moved him to show the white flag of defeat.

"Let us call a halt," he said in a long letter to Mr. Morgan.

"You started it," replied the latter briefly, and the next day, the *Herald's* first page looked like a circus handbill.

Then came the most trying time of all, for war seemed near, indeed. From the English news agency, Mr. Gorson received columns of dispatches beginning, "We learn," and "It is announced upon excellent authority." His cable bills swallowed his profits and cut wide swaths into his capital, and, meanwhile, his rival appeared to flourish as the green bay tree. But with the traditional doggedness of the true-born Briton, he hung to his small type, his "We understand" phraseology, his belated cables, and his insufficient imagination. Finally, finding himself utterly unable to rival the lurid sensationalism of Mr. Harris Morgan's dispatches, he undertook the herculean task of exposing their mendacity. Day after day, he read and re-read the *Herald's* telegrams in search of blunders, and with pleasing frequency, he found them. Once, in fact, he succeeded in completely disproving a story regarding the purchase of mules in Bulgaria by the Spanish Minister of War. Next morning, elated by his victory, he opened the *Herald* with a smile of exceeding contentment. Across the first page, in county fair handbill letters as large as the characters upon a signboard, was the legend, "War Declared!"

"It's a bloody falsehood!" said Mr. Gorson to himself with a smile. "The dispatches say nothing of it!"

And then, like a lawyer annihilating his rival's case, he seated himself at his desk and penned a vigorous and highly sarcastic expose of the story's untruth. "We are agreeably surprised," he began, "to note that our contemporary has established a mental telepathy cable line between this colony and the land of our esteemed brethren, the Yankees."

Thus, for half an hour, Mr. Gorson poured out the vials of satire upon the head of Mr. Harris Morgan. After he had carefully corrected his manuscript, he folded it neatly, called his black copy boy and dispatched it to the composing-room with an order that it be set up in minion and triple-leaded.

Just as the copy boy withdrew, a messenger rushed up the stairs with a thin blue cable envelope. Leisurely opening the end, Mr. Gorson drew out the enclosed "flimsy" and spread it before him. This is what he read:

A — 23 — bulletin
London, Tuesday, 7 P.M.

Times, Kingston
War declared today. Two hundred words follow.

R. T.

Four times Mr. Gorson read this crushing document. Four times he weighed its every word, and four times he shuddered as a glimpse of the future flashed across his mind. Dank it was, and dark and ill, and in the distance, he saw the *Times* office with the red flag of the auctioneer fluttering over the doorway.

"It means ruin!" he sighed. Ruin—absolute!—unless—"

Suddenly, he raised his head, for an inspiration had seized him.

Would not Morgan listen to reason?

The *Herald* belonged to the *non est* Mr. FitzJames Fitz-Hugh. Morgan's interest was merely that of an employee. His "scoops" increased the paper's profit, but they did not add to his salary. Foolish youth! Would he not listen to reason?

I could afford to give him a hundred guineas, thought Mr. Gorson.

He may knock you down, whispered a small voice within him.

I'll risk it, he decided at last.

The *Herald's* business office was in a little one-story brick box at the corner of Harbour and Queen Streets. The editorial rooms and printing department were a block northward on Queen Street. As he passed the former place, on his way to the latter, Mr. Gorson saw a huge bulletin on the doorside signboard. Thus it read: "The *Herald's* exclusive announcement that war is declared between Spain and the—"

Mr. Gorson hurried on to the house wherein the *Herald* was manufactured. As he turned into the dark doorway leading to the editorial rooms, Mr. Harris Morgan rushed into his arms.

"Hello, old man!" exclaimed Mr. Morgan, dragging the proprietor of the *Times* along with him. *"Wie gehts?"*

"You are on a journey?" suggested Mr. Gorson feebly.

"Sure!" replied Mr. Harris Morgan, with a smile of wild happiness. I've got an offer to cover the war for the *New York Star!* I catch the ten-five for Port Antonio and go aboard the dispatch boat at five. I'm done with Jamaica! Thanks be—"

"And the *Herald?*"

"D__n the *Herald!*" replied Mr. Morgan piously. "It don't belong to me!"

He sprang into a cab and was off.

"Good luck to you!" shouted Mr. Gorson after him.

The Point of the Story

"Therefore shall his calamity come suddenly;
suddenly shall he be broken without remedy."
—Proverbs, VI, 15

MISS WHITING read the sprawling headlines slowly, and her glance as slowly drifted to the first paragraph of the story beneath then. Then she let the paper flutter to the floor and looked sadly out of the window.

There was an arrogant, brazen effrontery in the black type that stung her like a blow on the cheek. Its staring ugliness held the eye, and its dirty blackness seemed like a smirch. Miss Whiting had followed the uncouth letters, not because they attracted her, but because there was that in them that vexed her and made her angry and unhappy.

With the deadly terseness of a newspaper head, they proclaimed to all the world that dishonesty had crept into the government of the city. Men giving pavement contracts, they said, were abstracting unearned money from the treasury in amounts sufficient to make them rich, and the officials whose duty it was to guard against such things were criminally negligent. One among the latter was singled out as the man responsible for the "steals," and it was cunningly hinted that his lack of watchfulness was due to the fact that he shared the plunder.

This man was twice mentioned by name in the black headlines. "Killis," they said in one place, "feigns ignorance—the young director of Public Works proves an apt pupil of the machine." Then they went on to elaborate upon this charge, and, lower down in the body of the story, it was cleverly made to appear that he had endeavored to shield the alleged thieves by refusing to discuss their peculations. Then there was a sarcastic paragraph about his previously "clean" record—with the "clean" in quotation marks—and, at the end, an eloquent demand for an investigation.

Miss Whiting read no further than the first paragraph, for it is not pleasant to have one's guests called names, and the director of public works had promised to dine that night with the Whitings.

More than once, by many times, he had eaten the Whiting bread and salt. First, he had come as the guest of the head of the house, to discuss a matter which required the smoking of many cigars and the mention of many names. Next, he had come as visitor-in-ordinary to the whole family, and then, after a long and meditative smoke in his office, he had begun to wonder why he had come so often. By dint of much logical reasoning, he reached the conclusion that it was because Miss Whiting was the only girl in the United States—the only one, at any rate, that he had met—who knew enough about politics to discuss intelligently the difference between a ward and a precinct.

Miss Whiting, in the meanwhile, had begun to wonder why most women looked upon politics as a bore. In the abstract, she admitted to herself, there was little in it to interest anyone, but then, when Killis told of his plans and his fights and of the fights made against him, wasn't there human interest in the story, and personal interest, too? Miss Whiting thought of these things as she stood at the window with the paper and its black headlines in her hand, and they were in her thoughts when Killis walked in unannounced and saw her attempt to hide it in her music rack.

He came toward her with an appealing look, and she saw that his face was white and drawn.

"I am sorry," he began confusedly, "that you have been reading that—"

Miss Whiting flushed slightly and feigned not to have

heard him.

"You are late," she said, proffering her hand.

Killis glanced at the clock.

"No; I am not late," he replied slowly. "I am early, purposely—to make excuses."

He took a seat by the window and his gaze dreamily wandered to the music rack.

"Dinner is almost ready," said Miss Whiting nervously. "Can't you stay?"

Killis sat in silence for a moment, as if the question were one difficult of answer.

"Oh, I could, I suppose," he said at length, "but I think that I had better not."

Miss Whiting simulated lack of comprehension.

"You see," he went on, "I had made certain plans, and fate has spoiled them. I had intended to tell you why I—"

"Fate is not irresistible," observed Miss Whiting.

Killis paused.

"There is no need," continued Miss Whiting, "to be afraid of it."

"It's not fear!" exclaimed Killis, rising, as if in anger. "It's shame! Shame is more than fear. I came here to tell you—and I will tell you—that I love you, love you! But, as I entered your house, I found you reading—that! Do you think I could ask you to share such a life as—as that says I have been leading? Would it be manly—or decent?"

Miss Whiting turned to the window and looked out upon the passing crowd. Then she came to where Killis sat, with his head resting upon his fists, and laid her hand upon his shoulder.

"You didn't mean all of that?" she said softly.

Killis stretched forth his arm and drew her to his side.

"I meant all of it," he answered. "I meant that I love you, love you, love you. I meant that I have waited for the chance to tell you, in fear that what has happened was coming. I meant that it has made me lie awake at night and regret that I ever met you. And, now, I want to tell you — and to say goodbye to you."

Miss Whiting stole a glance at Killis, but he looked away. Then he arose and paced up and down the room in silence. Miss Whiting watched him.

"I, too," she said in a low voice, "have something to tell —"

Killis stopped with a start and came toward her.

"You love me?" he whispered.

"Yes," answered Miss Whiting simply; "I love you."

"But — that?"

"Why should I heed what people say of you?" replied Miss Whiting, almost angrily. "What do I care for such — for such — blackmail? Isn't it enough that I know that you are innocent? Why snould you hang your head as if you were a convicted criminal? Why should you — can't you —"

"No, I can't," replied Killis, turning away from her.

"You must!" exclaimed Miss Whiting.

"But I can't," answered Killis pitifully, "because —"

"Because?"

"Because I have no right to let you talk to me like that. I should have been a man and remained silent, but I couldn't, and so you have —" He paused and gazed dreamily out of the window. "But you don't know all of it! You don't know why I should have kept silence. You don't know why I should not have come to you. You don't — you can't know that — what that says — is *true!*"

And, just at that moment, in came Miss Whiting's mother, all smiles, to welcome Killis and to announce that dinner was ready and waiting.

A Double Rebellion

THE SEÑOR Enrique Tarazona became a revolutionist through no fault of his own—unless it can be considered a fault to yield to the narcotic caresses of the Caribbean dawn-wind.

As a licensed pilot on and along the coast of Yucatan, it was his duty, perhaps, to remain awake under every and all circumstances. But duty, in most parts of the world, is largely modified by custom, and on the coast of Yucatan, it is the custom of the licensed pilots to retire to the chart-room for a brief cat-nap when, after fourteen hours at the wheel, they bring a banana steamer into the safe roadstead of an out-port.

This custom has many defenders, and the Señor Tarazona thought it an admirable one. Consequently, it was with a feeling of virtuous satisfaction that he curled up on the captain's chart table as the steamer *Choctaw* dropped anchor in the harbor of Santa Dolores. On the wharf, he knew, there were ten thousand bunches of green bananas, and five hours, he calculated, would be required to transfer them, in surf boats, to the swinging platforms over the *Choctaw's* sides.

While these five hours were passing, the captain and officers of the *Choctaw* would be drinking limeade ashore, the men of the crew would be dozing in the shade of the forward awning, the fifty black stevedores would be perspiring and struggling with the bunches of bananas, and the pair of yellow supercargoes would be shouting in forceful and stentorian manner.

During the night trip up from Belize, the Señor Tarazona had remained at the wheel while all but the quartermaster and the engineer's men slept. Through the treacherous maze of inshore channels and murderous shoals and rocks,

he had guided the *Choctaw* to Santa Dolores. As she thread-
ed her way in and out, the stevedores snored in the moonlight, the captain snored in the chart-room, and the supercargoes snored on bundles of coconut bags beneath the
bridge. Now, when all of these gentlemen were preparing
to work or to direct work or to play, it was time for the Señor Tarazona to sleep. This, as has been stated, he did.

Though it was in violation of the regulations made and
provided, and the owners stormed when they heard of it,
the captain of the *Choctaw* took all at his officers with him
when he went ashore in the first surf boat that put out to
the steamer. As soon as he was out of sight, the men of the
crew stopped their labors to take a stealthy dip in the blue-
green water over the stern, and before long, no one remained aboard but the chief machinist, who tinkered with
the boilers; the pair of supercargoes, who yelled and
fumed; the perspiring stevedores, who labored; and the Señor Tarazona, who slept.

It was while the fire-room gang was playfully ducking
the cook beneath the overhang that Brown, the senior supercargo, struck Montague, a stevedore, with a hammer.
Brown, because of his quarter-section of Caucasian blood,
looked upon Montague, a pure Ethiopian, as a lower animal. But Montague, being a citizen of the island of Jamaica
and a British subject, regarded himself as the superior of
any mere Mexican in Mexico. Consequently, he was much
incensed when Brown fined him half a day's pay for dropping a bunch of bananas overboard, and Brown was much
incensed when he went on strike. Consequently, also,
Brown struck him with the hammer and he fell to the deck.

What happened during the next few moments is but in-
distinctly remembered by those who were there. It is
known, however, that all work stopped in an instant, and
that in another instant, Brown and his fellow supercargo
fell overboard. It is also known that a half-dozen pistols

sprang from a half-dozen pockets, that the chief machinist down in the fire-room was dragged on deck and forced to walk the plank, that the propeller of the *Choctaw* turned and the men of the crew swam like eels out of the wash, that the vessel slowly gained headway and backed toward the open sea, and that the Señor Tarazona slept through it all.

When he awoke, he found the *Choctaw* pounding about in the long swell off the port entrance. On the forward deck, Montague, the stevedore, with his head bandaged with bagging, was making an impassioned harangue. As he spoke, his hearers shouted "Vive!" and "Hear, hear!" and "Hooray!" The Señor Tarazona, rubbing his eyes blankly, staggered, as if groping his way to the bridge rail, and stared at the assemblage.

"Come down!" commanded Montague, the first to espy him.

"Your officers?" gasped the Señor.

"Overboard!" replied Montague. And the others laughed loudly.

Then it was explained to the Señor that the party of fifty colored gentlemen before him, having become weary of the yoke of oppression, had resolved to throw it off. As natives of the island of Jamaica and as British subjects, they said, it was their duty to thus stand up for their rights. Merely as a lesson to their oppressors—to wit, Mr. James Brown, supercargo; Mr. R. Lopez, his colleague; the officers and men of the steamer *Choctaw,* and the Belize-American Fruit Company, Limited—they had decided to seize the said steamer and later to take possession of the said company's wharves, buildings, docks, channels, and other property at the out-port of Don Raphael, ten miles up the coast.

"We want you," said Montague, in Jamaican-Mexican-English-Spanish, "to take us there. If you throw us down"—American slang comes down on the banana boats — "woe betide you."

"You are pirates!" exclaimed the Señor Tarazona.

"We are!" replied Montague. And, with the muzzle of a pistol thumping his ribs, the Señor took his place at the wheel.

In charge of the engines of the *Choctaw* was a gentleman who had made two trips between Kingston and Liverpool as a stoker on an Atlas liner. Thus he had obtained an interesting, albeit limited, knowledge of steam gear, and with this knowledge to guide him, he set about directing the half-dozen men told off to help him. In ten minutes, they had shoveled two and a half tons of coal into the *Choctaw's* furnaces and the wheels began to turn. Then, with the muzzle of the pistol still thumping his ribs, the Señor Tarazona steered the *Choctaw* out to sea, around Coconut Point, and westward toward the out-port of Don Raphael.

As may be supposed, there was much excitement at Santa Dolores when the crew of the steamer and the supercargoes were picked up, half drowned, by the surf boats, and very much more excitement when the steamer herself backed out to sea. For a while, the captain, the officers, the resident agent, and the local police stood upon the roof of the banana shed and gazed dumbly. Then the resident agent bethought him that, in the mouth of the creek that bounded the town on the west, lay a steam launch. In this launch, there stood, rusting, a duplex engine and a machine gun without sights. Straightway, in order that the machine gun might be exercised upon the fleeing *Choctaw,* water and fire were brought to the engine, and the erstwhile chief engineer of the steamer took off his coat.

But before steam was up and the propeller churned the water, the *Choctaw* had arrived off the striped and lightless lighthouse that marked the out-port of Don Raphael. As her engines stopped and she drifted shoreward on the heavy swell, Montague, the stevedore, and the more crafty of his brethren, held a conference in the cabin for the purpose of deciding upon a plan of attack.

It was their unanimous conclusion that a fight at close quarters was the only kind in which they would have the advantage, and, in consequence, the Señor Tarazona was called below from the bridge and directed to steer the *Choctaw* between the twin shoals at the harbor mouth and into the transparent little puddle that formed the harbor. Once inside, it would be in order to make for the landing, swarm ashore, take the warehouses by storm and put the company's representatives to flight. Then might come a safe retreat with the spoils, and happiness ever after. The dark-skinned Anglo-Jamaican, be it known, reckons no further in the future than the morrow.

The Señor Tarazona made strenuous objection to this plan, because, as he said, he had no relish for a death by hanging. But as those to whom he presented his objection made no other reply than to offer him the alternative of death by bullet wound or drowning, he quite willingly ascended to the bridge again and took the wheel.

It was a difficult passage, the entrance to Don Raphael harbor, and with a pistol pointing toward him from either side, the Señor Tarazona attempted it with many a tremor. Throwing the wheel hard to starboard, he pushed the bridge telegraph down to "Full Speed Ahead," and as the ship beneath him gained motion, he pulled his cap down over his eyes and stared over the bows like a lookout in a fog. By the pink coral reef that formed the breakwater, and rigidly in the course marked by the end of Maria Point and the tall palm on the far shore, the *Choctaw* howled along. Then she entered the crook of the channel and bore down upon the twin shoals. Six times she swerved to port or starboard like a train rounding a curve. Then she wobbled uncertainly, and with a yell, the Señor Tarazona sprang to the telegraph and pushed the handle over to "Full Speed

Astern." But down in the engine-room, the bell rang three times in vain, for the gentleman who had learned steam engineering in the fire-room of the Atlas liner thought that three bells signified "Faster Ahead." So he ordered more coal in the furnace and more oil on the crankshaft, and while the amateur passers were wheeling the coal from the bunkers, and the amateur oilers were flooding the oil-cups, the *Choctaw* struck the port shoal with a shock that laid half of her passengers flat.

Montague, the stevedore-captain, who was the first to scramble to his feet, made an instant dash for the bridge.

"Traitor!" he shouted as he pounced upon the Señor Tarazona.

"Swine!" bellowed the latter in Castilian rage. And then he dropped into Jamaican-English: "Ze en-gians not stop! Ze—"

"Traitor!" shouted a dozen voices behind Montague.

"Hang him!" shouted one of them.

"Hang him!" repeated the others, savagely.

Now, the Señor Tarazona, as has been said before, had no relish for a death by the noose, and for this reason he begged loudly for a pardon, and when he saw that it was not forthcoming, for a reprieve.

"I take her off ze shoal!" he protested excitedly. "By five minutes, I do eet!"

"Hurry!" said Montague magnanimously.

Then the Señor Tarazona signaled again for "Full Speed Astern," and, after a proper interval, during which the gentleman who had learned steam engineering in the fire-room of the Atlas liner was told the meaning of three bells, the *Choctaw's* crank shaft turned over slowly toward the left. Just as the vessel began to struggle with the shoal and the speed indicator pointed to fifty revolutions, one of the amateur sub-assistant engineers dropped a handful of waste into the apparatus which served as a governor for the engines. Then came a loud report, a piece of steel tore through the engine-room hatch, the *Choctaw* trembled and the engines ran away.

There are those who hold that the engines of a steamship have souls, like race horses, and in support of this principle they point out the fact that when scrap pile engines break bounds, they cause more trouble—like senile cab horses—than high-strung and blooded stock. The engines of the *Choctaw* were built on the Clyde when steam engineering was a rudimentary art, and in consequence they were fearfully and wonderfully made. So when their governor—which corresponded to the conscience—was mutilated by the handful of waste, they gaily and energetically set out to tear themselves to pieces.

Like the second hand of a clock, the speed indicator rushed 'round and 'round, until it reached the limit of its possible travels, and like the paddle of an old-time sternwheeler, the propeller of the *Choctaw* heaved, and thrust and splashed and billowed the water under the stern. When the governor broke, the amateur stokers were congratulating themselves upon the fact that the boilers held twenty pounds of steam more than the printed notice by the gauges said that they could hold. When the speed indicator lurched forward and the propeller grew excited, the amateur stokers swarmed up the hatchway and left the steam gear of the *Choctaw* to its fate.

To a man who has passed through a South American earthquake and hurricane, the terrors of a runaway marine engine may seem laughably trivial, but in the eyes of the man familiar with only the ordinary convulsions of nature, they are exceedingly nerve-racking. The engines of the *Choctaw,* after the first wild throbs, buckled down to their work with a will. Faster and faster they spun 'round, and louder and louder they thumped and roared, and wilder and wilder were the spurts of the screw. Soon the ship swayed from side to side, and the decks trembled, and the funnel creaked, and the guy ropes lashed each other like the strands of a whip.

And then, as if she were a bucking bronco tugging at a foot-rope, the *Choctaw* tore at the coral sand of the shoal and her nose plowed it and pounded it and ground it into dust. Suddenly, with a jar that sent the terrified rebels sprawling and hurled the Señor Tarazona against the swinging wheel, the keel slid from the sand like a cork popping from a bottle, and the *Choctaw* sprang backward. In a minute, she was tearing stern-foremost toward the open sea. As she flew by the pink coral reef that formed the breakwater, something broke in her steering gear and a flying piece of steel splashed the water half a mile ahead. Then the wheel was torn from the Señor Tarazona's grasp, the rudder snapped over to starboard, and the *Choctaw* began to gallop around in a circle—with her bow where her stern should have been.

Thereupon—being believers in occultism and obeah—the gentlemen rebels on her deck gave way to sickening fear. Montague, the stevedore, who had been knocked down by the first lurch, arose unsteadily, and his face was gray with terror. His compatriots and fellow-rebels, even more scared than he, rushed for the bow—which was now the stern—and measured the chances of escape by jumping overboard. But the *Choctaw* was now half a mile from shore and the transparent green water was the home of sharks, and so they huddled along the rail and quaked and trembled and regretted that they had not been contented with their lot. Now and then, something broke down in the engine-room and the air was burdened with the hiss of steam and the clank of loosened steel. Following one of these accidents, the rudder switched suddenly from starboard to port and the Choctaw went over on her beam end so far that the starboard rail was nearly awash. Then the gentlemen rebels gave up all hope, and, with loud and pleading voice, called upon the gods of all the cults of obeah to save them for lives of future repentance and lawfulness.

The Señor Tarazona, alone among the *Choctaw's* passengers, seemed unconcerned. When the rudder went over, he dived into the chart-room, and here, with a cigarette in his mouth, he waited until the engines should stop, for, by virtue of his superior education, he knew that steam boilers, to furnish steam forever, require perpetual stoking. Since the amateur sub-assistant engineer had dropped waste into the governor, there had been no feeding of the furnaces. Consequently, the engines must run down before long, and in the meanwhile—what was the need of worrying? The steering gear was useless, the rebels were paralyzed with fear; there were no means of salvation and no fear of sudden death by bullet. Patience, plainly, was the virtue to be practiced, and the Señor Tarazona, being a Mexican, was patient.

Even as he had inwardly predicted, the engines of the *Choctaw* ran down. Less and less did the propeller lash the water, and fewer and fewer grew the jolts in the engine-room. But the fear of the dark-skinned passengers did not decrease in like proportion and when at last the screw made a farewell spurt or two, and settled into motionlessness, they were still gray with terror and still anxious to put the *Choctaw* from their sight and touch.

In this desire, fortunately, a vagrant gulf wind aided them. As the *Choctaw* came to a stop and settled into the swing of the ground swell, a puff of air came out of the east and bore her gently shoreward. Then came more breeze and soon her bottom lightly touched the shelving sand that marked the seaward end of the beating surf. As she stopped, the Señor Tarazona sauntered from the chart-house, lighted a fresh cigarette, and watched the rejoicing revolutionists dive over the side and scramble through the surf to the shore. As the first one reached the beach and rushed into the thicket of bananas and crotons and disappeared from view, there came tearing around Maria Point a steam launch filled with men. In the bow of the launch was a rusty machine gun, and one of the men stood by it with his hand upon the crank.

"Don't shoot!' yelled the Señor Tarazona in Jamaican-English and Mexican-Spanish as the muzzle bore down upon him. "I save ze ship! Ze insurrectos run!"

And even as he spoke, the last of the band was swallowed by the shade of the bananas and crotons.

Hurra Lal, Peacemaker

HURRA LAL'S father, Moffut Lal, came from India in a big ship that struck many storms and rolled and pitched dreadfully, and so made him — Moffut Lal — very ill indeed, for he was an up-countryman from Lucknow-way and had never seen the sea until he went aboard at the Calcutta dock; but of all this, Hurra Lal knew nothing, except by hearsay, for, in truth, he was not born until four or five years after the ship landed Moffut Lal, his father, and his father's wife, at Kingston, in Her Britannic Majesty's island-colony of Jamaica, in the West Indies, and until after his father, Moffut Lal, had become a practiced and valued driver of mules upon the Long Valley banana plantation, on the south slope of the low, clumsy, lazy-looking mountain which skirts the northeast coast.

Hurra Lal was born in a house built of wattles and palm-thatch, far up on the mountain, near the bare crest, and when he was old enough to stray away from the doorsill, he used to climb to the flat, open space beyond the last row of banana trees — it was like the top of a bald man's head — and gaze out over the blue-green Caribbean. On fair, clear days, there was a little strip of dark, pinky-purple along the line where the sea met the sky, and once Hurra Lal heard the overseer *sahib* tell a couple of other *sahibs* — they were gringos and marveled — that the strip of pinky-purple was Cuba. But this information was of little value to him, for he was uncertain whether Cuba was a ship, a field, a house, or an animal.

By and by, he came to the conclusion that it was a snake. His father talked much of snakes, and told dreadful tales of their doings overseas in India. There were no snakes in Jamaica, because, as Moffut Lal said, the mongoose had eaten all of them. This, too, puzzled Hurra Lal, for the mongoose was a little animal that stole chickens, and it seemed impossible that it should swallow a thing as large as the long pinky-purple snake at the edge of the sea.

Nevertheless, he accepted and believed all that Moffut Lal told him, for there were many things that seemed queer, and it was easier and more satisfactory, in the long run, to believe them offhand than to investigate and doubt them.

For instance, there was the matter of the Queen. Moffut Lal said that she was a great white *memsahib,* with a gold crown on her head, and that she lived in a place called England, far beyond the sea. Hurra Lal sometimes peered across the waters in hopes of seeing her, or, at least, of catching a glimpse of the gold crown upon her head, but except in the early morning, when the sun rose, he saw no gold. But this did not dispel his belief in her existence, nor in the story that she wore a gold crown.

He knew of his own knowledge that the Queen was of high and mighty estate, for many of the white *sahibs,* at certain seasons of the year, met to eat and drink, and when the drinking began, they would arise and cry out to their God to save her. Also, at other times, the young of the *sahibs* sung songs to the same effect, and always, when her name was mentioned, or the music of the song was made, the *sahibs* took off their hats. So, too, when Moffut Lal took Hurra Lal to Kingston to meet his uncle, who came in a ship from India, he saw many soldiers, and one afternoon, when they were assembled in great multitudes in a broad, flat field, and the flags waved and the captain *sahibs* rode up and down on horses, the soldiers, when they heard the Queen's name, called out loudly, "Rah, rah, rah!"

In some way, Hurra Lal began to associate any mention of the Queen with the soldiers. For one thing, whenever they marched along the coast road, there was much playing of the music of the song wherein the God of the white men was called upon to save her. Also, whenever a big ship with guns dropped anchor in the roadstead, or in the little, round west harbor at Port Antonio, the soldiers on her decks—at least, they were white men who appeared and acted as soldiers—made the music of the same song each evening as the sun went down. So Hurra Lal looked upon soldiers in general as singers of this song, and whenever he saw them, he half expected to hear it.

In truth, it was rather seldom that Hurra Lal really saw the soldiers, for they marched along the coast road only occasionally, and it was only occasionally that Moffut Lal took him to the places where they congregated. Perhaps, if he had been more familiar with them, he would have known that they had many other duties and very many other pastimes besides carrying guns and singing the song and crying, "Rah, rah, rah!"

Moffut Lal said that, at home, in India, there were many soldiers, white and brown, and that when six more years had passed, and a certain number of shillings had been amassed, he and Hurra Lal, and Hurra Lal's mother and the baby would return to India, and there, in a snug little bazaar of their own outside the gate of the fort, they would sell the soldiers trinkets and jewels to send home to their wives and sweethearts in England. Moffut Lal said that the white soldiers were worthy of all admiration, but that the brown ones were sometimes naught but haughty upstarts. In Jamaica, there were mainly white soldiers, though over in Kingston there were a few who were coal black. These, said Moffut Lal, belonged to Her Majesty's Royal West India Regiment—whatever that might be. Moffut Lal did not like them, for, as he said, it was not meet that they should affect such fine clothing as they did.

In the course of time, Moffut Lal—or, at least, certain of his friends—came to dislike them—and the white soldiers, too—even more. It all began in the matter of the tax-gatherers. There was a tax upon idle land—or "ruinate," as it was called—and another tax upon land fit for pasture for cattle, and another tax upon land planted or grown in guinea grass, and still another and yet larger tax upon land under full cultivation. The *sahib* who owned the Long Valley banana plantation had given to each head of a family in his service a bit of land large enough for a thatch house and a garden patch, with provision that the tax should be paid by the occupant. As idle land, it was taxed at a farthing for each acre. As pasture, the tax was three farthings, and under guinea grass, the tax was a penny and a half. When yams were planted, and bananas, and huts were built, the tax-gatherer demanded thruppence—twelve times as much! The heads of families protested. Why should their labor be charged against them? Why should those in authority place a penalty upon industry? The tax-gatherer was either a knave or a fool.

One of the heads of families—Boora Dat, an old man with lean legs and a curling lip—called the others together and spoke to them. Should they submit? No, they answered, each louder than the other. Submission was for cravens; they would have none of it. Moffut Lal arose to counsel caution, but the others laughed at him. Was he a coward? Was he afraid? Perhaps he preferred to be oppressed? If so, there could be no objection, but cowardice—

Moffut Lal said no more. What could a man do?

When the tax-gatherer came again, there was much excitement, and the *sahib* who was overseer, and the *sahib* who owned the plantation, made speeches to the heads of families, showing the wisdom of the law. But the heads of families would not hear them, though they loved and respected them greatly, and the tax-gatherer went away.

In seven days, he returned again—with a black constable—and then—bad luck and worse stars!—there was trouble. Several of the young men, in the pride of their

youth, hooted at him and called him names. He called upon the constable to arrest them. The constable walked toward them, and then—

Moffut Lal came home later and told of it with trembling
lips. There had been a scuffle, and much kicking and beating with clubs. The tax-gatherer had been struck in the face.
The constable had been put to flight. Moffut Lal, alarmed,
had counseled peace, but the young men were lost in their
madness, and they misnamed him coward, as before. Thus
he came away and left them to their madness, and all that
night he lay awake and feared for the morrow.

NEXT MORNING, the young men, swelled with vain-
glory, strode up and down, and called upon all brave men
to join them. Feeling shame—they could not tell why—
many of the older and wiser heads dropped into their
ranks, and then, of a sudden, Moffut Lal, who yet remained
at home—for there was no work that day in the banana
fields—heard loud noises and shouts, and, rushing out,
saw the mob throwing stones at the house of the overseer,
in the valley. There were many guns in the house, and the
overseer, on the veranda, fired one of them, and a young
man, Lua Din, dropped in his tracks. This so enraged the
others that they rushed upon the house, and soon they
were marching back through the fields with guns across
their shoulders and cartridges slung in belts about their
waists. The overseer lay wounded upon the veranda. It was
horrible.

And then the mob came to the house of Moffut Lal and
dragged him out with cries of "coward," and made him
take a gun and march up and down. Moffut Lal saw that all
of the heads of families were in the mob, and he knew that
the devils of battle were loose and that there would be no
reason until blood had been shed and houses burned, for
when the devils of battle enter into the hearts of men—

unless something marvelous happens—it is past time to talk to them. Blood, alone, will appease them.

In a wild, disorderly array, the men marched up to the crest of the low, clumsy mountain that rose from the beach—fifty strong—and Boora Dat, the captain, ordered that a *sanger*—which is a low stone rampart—be made. So, for hours, they worked feverishly, as if they were being pursued, throwing stones one upon the other and digging down into the hard dirt with their hands, and making gutters in the stone piles for their guns—and, in truth, they were being pursued, for when the tax-gatherer and the constable staggered into Port Antonio, there was great telegraphing to and fro, and great excitement, and in a few hours a company of black soldiers of Her Majesty's Royal West India Regiment were on a train which was being drawn by two engines, at top speed, up the steep slopes of the mountains between Kingston and the north coast.

So the men, at Boora Dat's commands, dug furiously, and the overseer lay on the veranda of his house and breathed slowly, and the soldiers in the train drew ever nearer and nearer, and the day wore on to night, and Hurra Lal wondered why Moffut Lal, his father, was away, and why his mother wept, and why there was no work in the banana fields. Toward evening, there came a rumor to the mountain that the soldiers had reached Port Antonio and would march down the coast road in the night. Tired and sore, the men under Boora Dat ceased their work upon the *sanger* long enough to send down into the valley for food, and after they had eaten it, they lay down on the cool, moist earth and some of them slept. But the most of them— and Moffut Lal was of this number—slept not at all, for the weight of a crime was upon them and they feared.

Down on the mountainside, in the home of Moffut Lal, Hurra Lal and his mother were awake. All night, Hurra Lal's mother prayed to the gods for the safety of Moffut

Lal, and for the end of the time of fear. Hurra Lal, at first puzzled and then alarmed, lay for a while in silence, in a corner of the wattle walls—thinking, pondering, wondering. By and by, the cool land breeze came over the valley and scurried among the banana trees and fanned him, and the ground insects ceased their chirrupping and the noises of the night died away, and he fell asleep.

WHEN HE awoke, the cold dawn was come upon the earth, and far to the eastward, the sky was growing gray. Hurra Lal stealthily arose, and seeing that his mother, too, had been overcome by weariness, crept out into the roadway and looked about. It was as still as if not a living creature were breathing. But, by and by, a big, red-gilled John Crow came along, flying low and flapping his wings, and then, behind him, came another. As they passed, swooping earthward in search of carrion, Hurra Lal thought that he heard a strange sound along the coast road. The coast road ran down the beach from Port Antonio until it came to the low, clumsy mountain, and then it verged inland and swung 'round in the valley, on the land side. The strange sound seemed to come nearer and nearer along the road—and, after a while, Hurra Lal recognized it. It was the tramp of marching men.

Suddenly, the sky in the east grew a bright red, and all the earth was lighted, and Hurra Lal saw that his ears had told him rightly. Far below him, on the white roadway, like shadows in the dawn mist, were two soldiers on horseback. Two others rode in the fields to either side of them, and, at a distance of three stone-throws behind them, marched a company of black soldiers of the Queen, with guns glinting in the morning light and a cloud of dust rising behind them. Their white officers strode along beside them. The peace of the Queen had been broken. Her sovereignty had been outraged. They were coming to exact her toll.

Stealthily, with crouching steps, Hurra Lal dived into the clump of dripping crotons behind the house and set out up the mountainside. Up through the dense undergrowth he climbed, over fallen banana trees, and wrecked palms, and tangled creepers and damp, clammy ferns. Then, emerging into the open, he scampered over boulders and across rain-dug ditches and stump holes, ever up, up, up, for on top of the mountain was Moffut Lal, his father, and the soldiers in the valley bore guns that might hurt him. So Hurra Lal, breathless and scared and thorn-scratched, ran uphill to warn him.

At the top of the mountain, Moffut Lal and the other men—the heads of families and the hot-headed youngsters—were darting about excitedly. Far below, in the valley, they had seen the glint of steel, and though they did not confess it one to the other, they were afraid. The Queen was merciless to her enemies. She had caused them to be slain in startling ways overseas in India. There was the way of binding to the cannon's mouth. There was the way of hanging by a rope. And then there was the way of shooting in the open with the rifle. It was not a pleasant business.

But Boora Dat laughed at them, and, in shame, they made ready.

"Lie low," he said loudly, "and shoot low. Aim for the knees."

Moffut Lal crawled into a corner of the *sanger* and laid his gun across the stones.

"God forgive me for what I do this day," he whispered to the dawn. And, in the hearts of most of the others, there was the same prayer.

Meanwhile, Hurra Lal scrambled across the loosed rocks and leaped across the ditches. Down in the valley, the soldiers of the Queen had halted. Soon they spread out in a long line, and then they separated each from the others, more and more, and drew nearer. They were coming.

Hurra Lal, pausing for breath, turned to look at them. A bugle call leaped across the distance, and Hurra Lal started anew. In a moment, he stopped to look back again. They were nearer. He could see their belt-plates and their shiny black faces. Again he ran forward: he was nearer the *sanger* on the crest: he slunk along in the shadows and the ditches. They might see him and shoot him.

Suddenly, his foot caught in a tangled vine and he pitched forward into a ditch. Time seemed to stop and the sky to grow dim. A clump of lilies at the edge of the ditch spun 'round queerly and melted into a pinkish haze, like a ray of light from a red sun, with millions of motes dancing about in it. Hurra Lal lay still for a while, and then, slowly, the haze melted and the lilies were there again, and, rubbing the dirt from his chubby face, he arose and peeped through the tangled stems.

What he saw made his little heart thump wildly. He held his breath until his breast fairly ached. The soldiers were within a stone's throw. They would catch him and kill him!

Suddenly, from up the mountainside, came a loud, tearing sound, and then a long, crawling whistle close to his ears. He ducked his head without at first knowing why. Then came another sound and another whistle, and he lay low. Boora Dat and his men were firing.

A tall white man rushing ahead of the soldiers spun 'round and clapped his hand to his shoulder. As he did so, his shoulder grew red, and the soldiers gave a loud shout and rushed by him. But two dropped out of the line to help him. Some were far away to the right, some were to the left; some were coming directly toward the ditch wherein Hurra Lal lay. They came singly, each for each, bounding from cover to cover. All were straining to their uttermost, rifles in hand and eyes aflame. They were soldiers at their work, and they wished to have it done and over. It was not pleasant work.

There came a red-faced captain *sahib* with a sword, somewhat ahead of them. Hurra Lal, breathless with fear, watched him through the weeds. Suddenly, he stopped and called "Halt!," and a bugler beside him blew a blast, and all of the men stopped, and then the red-faced *sahib* said something, and the bugler blew another blast, and the soldiers dropped to the ground and began to crawl uphill, like babies, from stone to stone and ditch to ditch. Hurra Lal was trembling like a palm in the dawn wind; perspiration stood out upon his brow.

One of the soldiers was coming directly toward him, on hands and knees, with his rifle under his arm. The man crawled like a snake. Surely he was a snake—of the kind known to Moffut Lal. A snake in human form! It was magic!

Hurra Lal cried aloud in terror, and then, just as there came another crash from up the mountainside and another shrill whistle overhead, he sprang from the ditch and waved his chubby little hand aloft, and yelled with all the power of his lungs:

"God save the Queen! God save the Queen!"

It was the soldiers' cry, and maybe they would spare him in consideration of his crying it.

"God save the Queen!"

Again he shouted, and the red-faced captain *sahib* stopped short and stared at him.

"God save the Queen!"

Hurra Lal once more repeated the cry in the strange, queerly-precise tones of the brown child struggling with the speech of the white man.

And, from up the mountainside, there came another cry—a long cry, as of a man in mortal terror.

"Spare the child!" came the cry. "Spare the child!"

"Halt!" shouted the red-faced captain *sahib*.

But Moffut Lal came bounding down over the boulders

and the ditches, his muscles swelled in strain and his face gray with terror,

"Spare the child!" he cried again, springing almost into the arms of the astonished captain *sahib,* and then, from above, came other cries. "Spare the child! Spare the child!" They were cries for mercy for the defenseless, but they were also—though this was never admitted—cries of surrender, and those who made them knew in their hearts that they were afraid.

Boora Dat—his eyes blazing and his clothes hanging in shreds—jumped to the ridge of the *sanger* and called them dogs and swine and cowards, but they still cried aloud and threw down their guns. Some of them he struck with his clenched fist and they fell, and others he dragged down and rolled on the ground. But they were tired of rebellion, for it was an unpleasant business, and there were wives and children down on the mountainside, and cannon and ropes and strange deaths, and so it came that they ran to the soldiers, crying "Spare the child!," and the red-faced captain *sahib* laughed, and the black soldiers of Her Majesty's Royal West India Regiment arose and stood at attention, and the white man whose shoulder was red was told off to belt them into line, and march them down the mountain—prisoners of war.

Hurra Lal rode on a palanquin made of crossed guns, shouting, "God save the Queen!"

Firing & a Watering:
An Episode of a South American Revolution

"If this were played upon a stage now, I could
condemn it as an improbable fiction."
— Fabian in *Twelfth Night*

NO ONE, of course, knew what it was all about—except, perhaps, Don Jamiee Cordova, who was in supreme command of the forces, and His Excellency the Señor Juan Casey y Torrijas, the admiral of the fleet—but this did not decrease the valor of the gallant soldiers and sailors of the insurgent army and navy, and neither did it diminish their belief that they were the victims of tyranny and oppression, and patriotism demanded that they fight for *el libertad*.

Bingham and Jones and Henderson, and the other Americans up at the coal mines, viewed the preparations for the conflict with a genial lack of interest, for revolutions had been so numerous for two or three years that it was becoming difficult to tell when one ended and the next began, and more difficult to discover the cause of each and the precise positions of the various generals and field marshals who seemed to be concerned.

First of all, there had been the rebellion in the interior, under the leadership of a half-breed named Huesca. Before long, Huesca appeared anew as the ally of the government forces and helped them defeat, capture, and hang a new insurrectionist, one José Borjas. Then he disappeared for a time. When he came into public view again, he was fighting cheek by jowl with Borjas' brother Fernando against the government leader, General Barbastro, and before long, he himself was captured and hanged, and Borjas' brother took to the mountains.

Now, it seemed, the revolutionary leader was Don Jamiee Cordova, a native and grandee of Spain and a gen-
tlemanly adventurer, who had come to Central America on
a carpet-bagging mission and had been defeated by General Barbastro three times "straight" in a series of sangui-
nary duels.

The coal mines were ten miles back from the sea, on the
left bank of the Rio Samala, and behind them rose the foot-
hills of the purple mountains in the distance. The Samala
was a muddy little stream that in the United States would
have been called a "crick," but, after a rain, it was naviga-
ble to small flat-bottom steamers, and upon craft of this
sort the coal taken from the mines was sometimes floated
down to the sea. But the greater part of it was hauled
southward across country on the Samala branch of the National Railroad, and so the Americans had come to pay little attention to the river and to look upon it only as an occasional haunt of big, brown crocodiles and a poor place
for bathing.

Now, however, they considered it more carefully, for at
its mouth, in the little harbor which appeared on the maps
as Port Caballos, there lay a blunt-bowed, flat-bottomed
little tub called the *Santa Rosa,* and His Excellency, the Señor Juan Casey y Torrijas, admiral of the fleet, was in
command of her. Fastened to her rail, on her port bow, was
a machine gun that had fallen to the Señor Torrijas as an
heirloom through an endless chain of revolutionist chiefs,
and on her decks, at ease beneath her awnings, lay two-
score swarthy, half-breed "jollies," smoking cigarettes and
contemplating the horizon. With the machine gun and the
"jollies," the Señor Torrijas hoped to convince the Americans up at the mines that it was their duty to lend him fifty
rifles—now reposing in their magazine—and to make the
revolutionary committee—which was the Señor and the
Don—a present of a thousand dollars in gold coin. It was

necessary, also, that this convincing be accomplished rapidly, for the government navy was steaming toward Port Caballos at the rate of five knots an hour, and when it arrived, there would be no time to deal with the *Americanos.*

Two days before, the Señor had visited them and set forth this idea, and they had rudely laughed at him and requested him, with coarse jokes and gibes, to remove himself from their presence within five minutes. He had then informed them that he would return, and now he was about to prove to them that he was a man of his word.

At noon, after the crew had eaten the midday meal and lighted fresh cigarettes, the *Santa Rosa* got under way, and before four o'clock, despite two breakdowns and a tilt with a shoal, she was within a mile of the mines. Then she slowed down and crept along the narrowing waterway, and around its countless bends and over its wicked shoals, until, at last, she rounded the marshy, palm-grown point at the seaward boundary of the mine compound. Ahead, on the right bank, lay the wilderness of derricks and smokestacks and the long, sprawling pile of culm, or refuse. This man-made mountain rose like a huge rampart separating the derricks and the river, and between it and the water's edge ran a muddy cart road. The river itself here narrowed to a width of less than a hundred yards and the insurgent flagship felt her way in toward the shore in the turbulent eight-foot channel.

As she came abreast of the lower end of the culm pile, a horseman appeared at its upper end, and in a moment he had galloped down and halted to survey her. The Admiral Casey y Torrijas, though the distance to the shore was scarcely more than a hop, skip, and jump, carefully leveled his marine glasses at the horseman and busily screwed the lens up and down to obtain a proper focus.

"An *Americano!*" he said to his aide.

In an instant, the horseman confirmed his verdict.

"Ship ahoy, there!" he shouted, making a megaphone of his hands. "What the deuce do you want?"

The admiral weighed his words before answering.

"Ve coom," he shouted, at length, "in ze name of *el libertad!*"

"Of who?" yelled the American.

"El libertad!" shouted the admiral, annoyed. The American was one of those that had spurned him with jibes a few days before. "We make ze request for ze loan of ze rifles and ze finanscheel assistant," he continued. "When we not get zem, we blow ze mine in ze atmosphere."

"You're trespassers!" shouted the American. "To the woods with you!"

Then he galloped up the road again and was joined by two others of his race. The three of them disappeared around the corner of the culm pile, and the admiral conferred with his aide regarding the beginning of the attack.

Very plainly, it would be dangerous to assault the mines from the front. True enough, the flagship was abreast of the derricks and the engine shanties, and a few rounds from the machine gun might knock the tops of them sky high. But near at hand was the culm pile, and it was high and long and massive. On account of it, it would be impossible to strike the lower parts of the buildings and impossible, also, to strike many of the *Americanos*. Besides, there were dents in the top of the pile, and some of these might conceal riflemen and gunners. It would not do to make a frontal attack against such odds. If there were to be odds, let them be on the other side.

The Admiral Casey y Torrijas decided, therefore, that it would be best to steam upstream two hundred yards to the upper end of the pile and there to land his "jollies" and storm the *Americanos'* flank. A short distance above, the stream made a bend to the right, and the guns of the flagship, from there, could be brought to bear upon the engines of the mines. Were one bullet to strike one boiler, and that boiler were to explode, the *Americanos* would be defeated, sectionally and scattering, beyond all hope of rallying.

So the flagship's stem wheel began to churn the water, and she set out, very slowly, upstream. As she came abreast of the middle of the pile, an *Americano* showed his head over the top of it and laughed an insulting laugh. Ten rifles covered him in an instant, but, before the triggers could be pulled, he was gone.

When the flagship came within twenty yards of the upper end of the culm pile, a queer thing happened. Back around the corner of the pile was a shed containing a donkey engine used to operate the rope of a derrick. Suddenly, steam came from the exhaust pipe above this shanty, and the engine within rattled. Then, like a long, attenuated sea serpent, a thin wire cable rose from the river. One end of it was fastened to the left bank and very evidently it had been immersed before the flagship hove in sight. Now the engine was pulling the right-hand end, and the wire rose from the water, becoming straight and taut as it rose and stretched across the stream from bank to bank, a few feet above the river level. It was a barrier intended to impede the flagship's progress—but the Admiral Casey y Torrijas was not worried. The flagship would charge it as a regiment of cavalry charges a redoubt and break it and tear it to pieces by the force of the impact!

Accordingly, the flagship was halted and allowed to drift downstream a few yards, and then the engine valve was opened wide, the stem wheel kicked furiously, and the warship bounded forward. Just as she did so, an *Americano* appeared around the corner of the culm pile, waving a white sheet. It was a flag of truce!—and the flagship halted to receive the *Americanos'* surrender. Plainly, they had been overawed, and as the truce-bearer came down to the water's edge and waved his flag, the crew of the warship cheered.

But the American's first words were not words of surrender, but of defiance.

"My dago friends," he said, "I have bad news for you." He came down to the bank and, being thus within a hundred feet of the admiral on the flagship, assumed a conversational tone. "Ahead of you," he said, "you will perceive a wire. It's a live wire, charged with ten thousand volts of electricity. This electricity is generated in the power house around the corner of the hill. No, it's no use; you can't hit it from here. Hey?"

The admiral had made an impatient remark.

"Well, as I was saying," continued the *Americano*—he was Henderson, the assistant superintendent—"this wire is a live one, and if your old tin-clad touches it, the juice'll explode your ammunition and you'll soar. Downstream"—the admiral turned round—"you will notice another wire of the same sort."

The admiral shaded his eyes with his hand, and, true enough, there was the wire at the lower end of the culm pile.

"This wire," continued the *Americano,* "is also a live one. If your old scow touches it, you'll never come down."

Then the *Americano* bowed low and climbed back over the pile.

"I have the honor," he said as he halted at the top, "to request your immediate surrender and to bid you good afternoon."

And he disappeared.

"*Diablo!*" muttered the admiral, turning to his officers. All of them had listened, spellbound, and now they were peering ahead and astern at the two wires with absorbed interest. In the bright tropical sunlight, the bare copper—the wires had been not long immersed—glittered and gleamed, and the vagrant river breezes made them tremble like high-strung springs. To the officers of the flagship, who were not well versed in natural science, the quiver of the wires betokened the presence of electric currents of ghastly power.

"Trapped!" moaned one of them, within hearing of the admiral.

"Trapped," repeated the latter, "but not defeated! A Castilian soldier never surrenders—either to man or devil! Ahead, the devil blocks us, but over there," pointing to the shore, "is man only. To the charge!"

"Bravo!" shouted the officers and the crew, and then cigarettes were thrown over the side, guns were loaded, cutlasses were unsheathed, and the rattling engines of the flagship began moving and pounding, and the flagship worked inshore, toward the muddy bank. By virtue of her three-foot draft, she was enabled to approach to within a few yards of the tangled weeds. Just as her bottom ground upon the sand and she came to a halt, her crew lined up on her starboard and fired a ragged volley at the skyline of the culm pile.

But, inasmuch as no *Americano* appeared or peered over it, there was no apparent damage, and so, without further waste of ammunition, the admiral gave the order for a landing, and ten of the gallant sailor soldiers sprang overboard and scrambled to the bank. Just as they were clear of the weeds and the admiral himself made a flying leap for *terra firma,* the shining barrel of what seemed to be a machine gun rose above a nick in the top of the pile, and a tiny American flag fluttered above it. The admiral stepped briskly out of the fire zone of the weapon and excitedly ordered the disembarkation to be hastened.

A second later, the thing gave a hoarse cough, as if it were clearing its iron throat, and then from its muzzle came a stream—not of bullets, or of shells, or of shrapnel, or of iron slugs—but of—what?—grayish, foul, filthy, mine water.

At the same instant, Messrs. Jones and Henderson sprang into view beside it and began sweeping it from side to side, as a gunner sweeps a machine gun. Back around the corner of the hill, in the pumping station of the mine, ten stokers, under Bingham, the chief engineer, were piling coal into the furnaces of the boilers that supplied steam for the giant mine pumps. From the pump house, over the rough ground, ran a line of six-inch hose. Up the landward side of the culm pile it ran, to the top, and at the top was a nozzle — and Jones and Henderson. According to the gauge back in the engine room, the nozzle was discharging ten thousand gallons of mine water a minute. According to the observation of Henderson and Jones, it was bowling over two revolutionists a second.

The admiral himself was the first to go over, and when, after a titanic struggle in the weeds and the water, he reached the deck of the flagship again, the stream caught him another time and he was hurled into the river. Before his warriors well knew what had happened to them, a dozen of them were sprawling in the shallow stream, and the flagship, moved by the impact of the watery cannonading, was rolling out toward midstream.

Just as she settled into the current, the gun on the culm pile ceased fire and, like wet sheep dragged out of a morass, the soldiers were hauled aboard and comforted. Then the flagship drifted downstream, helmless and helpless. A small reservoir of water from the strange gun had poured into the midship well that sheltered the ancient boiler, and the fire in its furnace was out. Dense clouds of steam rose from it, and the chief engineer wept aloud and tore his beard.

Of a sudden, the sodden admiral looked ahead and bethought him of the wire. In a few moments, the flagship would touch it —

And then? The *Americanos* were murderers and ghouls!

The rules of civilized warfare forbade such grisly tactics! It was assassination, not war! It was murder! The devil himself could invent no more revolting —

"Strike the flag!" commanded the admiral, breaking into tears. The crew dashed at the flagstaff and tore the revolutionist ensign from its fastenings. Half a dozen of them tore off such of garments as were white and waved them in token of surrender.

But the *Americanos,* very plainly, were not yet ready to talk of surrender. Not content with inventing new and devilish methods of murder, they were ready to violate every other rule in the book of civilized war. The white flag meant nothing to them. They would profane it and trample on it.

In thinking thus, the admiral was not wholly wrong, for, in truth, the *Americanos* had no intention of observing the regulations of the Geneva Convention. While the flagship drifted downstream and the crew made gigantic efforts to guide it inshore and aground and away from the deadly, glimmering wire, a corps of men, under Jones and Henderson, were connecting the hose with another length of canvas tube, which followed the line of the culm pile down stream. Near the lower end of the pile, there was another nozzle, and just as the helpless flagship came drifting inshore abreast of it, it was raised above the parapet of slate and coal dust, as the other had been, and Jones and Henderson arose and directed it toward the luckless warriors on the boat.

Then came another cough, another avalanche of dirty mine water, and another drenching, and soon the crew of the flagship struggled in the water again, and the flagship itself began to fill and sink. Like boys taking aim at toy soldiers, Henderson and Jones carefully and joyfully directed the stream at each individual sailor-soldier, from the admiral down. Some it struck full in the back, and they were hurled overboard as if they had been shot out of a gun. Others it struck about the feet, and they tripped and sprawled and rolled over the side, yelling and pleading for mercy. It was the most pleasant and fascinating sport that Jones and Henderson had ever encountered, and they enjoyed it to the full.

Soon, the flagship was in midstream, drifting toward the deadly wire again, and the men of her crew were struggling about her in the water. A few yards above the wire, she struck a snag and turned around so that her broadside faced the current. Then Jones and Henderson fixed the hose in place so that its stream would strike her amidships, and before long she began to fill and settle, and by and by she went down in six feet of water, helpless and deserted.

Past her, the half-drowned revolutionists floated on bits of driftwood and debris. The admiral, dripping and gasping, held fast to her life raft, which the water gun had hurled from her deck, and two of his officers swam toward the shore. Before long, the main body of the vanquished came to the wire, and because they were half dead and desperate and ready to grab at a straw or a red-hot iron, they forgot the deadly electricity and its cruel death, and with one accord, reached out for the gleaming strand of copper. When the pioneers lived, the others struggled after them, and soon the wire bore a heavy freight of sputtering, choking revolutionists, and Jones and Henderson, on the top of the culm pile, set up a camera and photographed them.

Suddenly, on the bank around the end of the pile, there was a hum of wheels, and the wire sank to the water level. The windlass had been unwound. Once more, then, the revolutionists struggled in the water and yelled and pleaded, and Jones and Henderson laughed. Then the windlass turned backward again, and the wire rose, and the revolutionists clung to it and fought for breath. A few seconds later, after most of them had begun to work their way, hand over hand, toward the shore, the windlass hummed again, and, once again, down went the wire. It was becoming cruel.

Four times the wire rose and fell, and then it remained high, and the revolutionists painfully toiled toward the opposite bank and disappeared in the jungle. As the last of them shook his fist at the *Americanos* across the stream and dived into the maze of foliage, a hoarse toot came from down the river, and soon the government gunboat *Gonzales* puffed up to the mine landing and her commander gazed at the stranded flagship in blind wonder.

"Vhere are ze *insurrectos*?" he asked of Jones and Henderson, who came down to greet him.

"They've taken to the woods," said Jones.

"Aha!" exclaimed the commander. "Zay scootle ze sheep and run vlien zay hear I am coming!"

Jones and Henderson laughed, and that evening, after dinner, they and Bingham showed him how it was done. He said that the *Americanos* were wonderful, indeed.

THE PASSING OF A PROFIT:
THE STORY OF A LOSING VENTURE

OF COURSE, there are Eminent Authorities who declare that a really successful betting system has never been and never will be invented, and that the chances at rouge-et-noir, faro, roulette, and *trente-et-quarante* will always remain four to three in favor of the bank; but a moment's thought will recall the fact that there were once, also, Eminent Authorities who maintained—and proved—that the earth was hexagonal, that iron ships would sink the moment they were launched, and that colds in the head might be cured—and caused—by witchcraft. The Eminent Authorities last named are dead now, and it is hard to find their graves, but those of the first class cited are yet numerous and enthusiastic, and because the mathematical doctrine of probabilities, which is a mighty and mysterious thing, is their main weapon, they are certain at all times of select and attentive audiences.

Nevertheless, a certain James R. Sarding, aided and abetted by one T. George Dixon, once proved them to be hopelessly wrong. The proving was performed upon the directors and stockholders of the Casino at San Mateo, and more particularly upon the Señor Enrique de Vegas, manager thereof, and although, in the end, the profit of Messrs. Sarding and Dixon was inconsiderable, the system which they employed operated perfectly.

Sarding obtained the secret of it from a Norwegian coal passer at Aden, who told wonderful lies and had a marvelous liking for Scotch whiskey. The whiskey, which served as fuel for the lies, was purchased by Sarding, and as he watched it disappear into the Norwegian's cavernous mouth, he listened. The story of the system is one of the things he heard.

For a year or more, he tested it in private, under all conceivable conditions. At first, it seemed to render the chances of the bettor no more than even, but, after a while, Sarding discovered a manner of improving it by playing at roulette upon combinations of the red and the number three, and, thereafter, the chances of the bettor arose from even to five to four, and then to seven to five, and to thirteen to seven.

When the last stage was reached, Sarding abandoned a plan which he had for selling condemned ships to the Haitian navy, and took passage from Baltimore on the tramp steamer *Toltec* for San Mateo, which is a town on the Mexican coast and the home of the San Mateo Casino, or American Monte Carlo. Sarding had heard of San Mateo as a favorite resort for American lambs and Mexican wolves. The former were in the habit of visiting the town during the winter, ostensibly for the benefits to be derived from the soft, tropical climate, but in reality for the benefit of the aforesaid wolves. Though the casino was a small, one-horse affair, and there was little big play, quite a few valuable American dollars had settled at San Mateo, and Sarding, being an American and patriotic, was desirous of repatriating them.

As the *Toltec* passed the Chesapeake capes, outward bound, Sarding made the acquaintance of Dixon, a tall, thin, beardless young man who wore ridiculous *"pince-nez"* and seemed to be suffering from a great depression of spirits. Dixon said that his father had put him aboard the *Toltec* while he (Dixon, Jr.) was in a state of alcoholic coma, and that he intended to travel in the West Indies until the three $100 banknotes in his inside pocket — which his relative had kindly provided — were gone. He ventured the further statement that he was "the family black sheep, or tribal skeleton," and that this was his fourth involuntary trip from home, and made several quotations from the works of

Rudyard Kipling to illustrate his story.

Him, Sarding at once hailed as a valuable ally—first, because of his money, and secondly, because of his general makeup and characteristics. On the third day out, an agreement was signed whereby the two engaged to pool their funds, and their possible profits; on the fifth day, Dixon was taught the method of operating the system, and on the sixth day, the pair landed at San Mateo and engaged quarters at the Hotel d'Europe.

The next morning, they were introduced to the Señor de Vegas, manager of the casino, as Americans of wealth and leisure by the Señor Juan Gonzalez, proprietor of the hotel. "Eet ees unfortunate," said the Señor de Vegas, "zat ze señors come not een ze season. Now zere ees not mooch American zshentlemen in ze ceety."

"Tut, tut!" said Dixon and Sarding, and then the trio walked along the veranda of the hotel until it met the veranda of the San Mateo Casino, which was next door, and there, the Americans stopped a moment to admire the gaudy tropical scenery and to light their after-breakfast cigars. Far below was the glimmering, shimmering gulf—a sea of diamonds and emeralds, and on the steep hillside, from the very gates of the casino to the water's edge, were dense thickets of short, sturdy palms and brilliant crotons. On the landward side of the casino was a huge coconut "walk" that reached up the hill, up, up, a waving riot of green, to the summit. On the giant slope from the beach to the crest, the casino and the hotel perched like a double chimney on a steep roof. Dixon and Sarding gazed for awhile in silence and admiration.

Then the Señor de Vegas discovered four distinguished friends—Don José Caballero, a member of the cabinet of his Excellency, the President of the Republic; Don Juan de Gato, a member of the National Railways Commission; the Señor Enrique de la Gastos y Bianca, governor of the city of

Tampico; and Count Leon Osterville, of the Belgian nobility.

Dixon recognized the count as one of the gentlemen who sat upon a pile of bagging at the dock and watched the *Toltec* unload, and the Señor Gastos y Bianca strangely resembled the man who sold clay images in the Plaza des Dames, down the hill in the town. But, for the present, the count was undoubtedly the Count Leon Osterville, a nobleman in search of amusement, and the Señor Gastos y Bianca was plainly the governor of the splendid city of Tampico, and the other gentlemen were exactly what they were, and so Dixon and Sarding said nothing, and the roulette wheel began to spin, and the game was on.

The Señor de Vegas was extremely sorry that the official croupiers—all of them—were off duty. There was but one—in fact, not away from San Mateo on vacation—for it was not the season—and this one, unfortunately, had broken his leg the night before. Perhaps the señors would wait until he recovered, or perhaps—would they permit the Señor de Vegas himself to play croupier? It would be a lark, a jolly lark—and, incidentally—this, the Señor de Vegas thought without speaking—it would be safer. Dealers were dumb dogs, and *Americanos* were crafty. It would be safer, certainly—and oh! it would be such a lark! The managing director of the casino in the croupier's seat! Dixon and Sarding laughed heartily. Also, they winked at each other when the Señor de Vegas and his friends were not looking their way.

"You honor us," said Dixon.

"*I* am honored," said Señor de Vegas.

And so the game began, and for two days and one night the wheel spun and spun, and Messrs. Dixon and Sarding staked their money upon combinations of the red and the number three. Late in the afternoon of the second day, the Señor de Vegas grew haggard and careworn, and his friends, the count, the dons, and the señor swore softly in Mexican-Castilian. The pile of dollars between Messrs. Dixon and Sarding was growing.

As the sun went down and the hill behind the casino grew scarlet and crimson, the Señor de Vegas pushed a little pile of gold toward Sarding and dropped a tear upon the spot beside him, whereon it had rested.

"Ze game moost stop," he whispered sadly. "Ze bank eez bo'st."

"Gentlemen," said Sarding, rising and calmly bowing to the Castilians, "my friend, Mr. Dixon, and myself must bid you good afternoon."

And, with all of the available cash assets of the casino at San Mateo in two bulky shot bags, Messrs. Dixon and Sarding walked along the veranda to the hotel, twice stopping to admire the reflection of the dying day in the shimmering blue-green of the sea far below them. Back in the main saloon of the casino, the Señor de Vegas was weeping, and his friends, the count, the señor, and the two dons, were comforting him.

"Swine!" said the count.

"Swine!" said the two dons.

"Ruined!" said the Señor de Vegas.

And in their room in the hotel, the swine laughed and made merry, for the system, despite the Eminent Authorities and the mathematical doctrine of probabilities, had been a success. The bank of the casino at San Mateo, the American Monte Carlo, was broken.

TWICE BEFORE dinner, Messrs. Dixon and Sarding counted their winnings. There were, in all, three thousand, four hundred and fifty dollars in silver, gold, and paper—a vast heap of rubbish which nearly filled Dixon's suitcase. Safely encased in that receptacle, the spoils were deposited in the middle of the floor of their room, and inasmuch as the next steamer away from San Mateo would not leave for six days, and there was not a trustworthy bank or safe-deposit vault within five-days' journey by land, they considered the matter of mounting guard. Finally, they determined to stand watches of eight hours, alternately, and after they had finished their meal and had drunk, in honor of their success, a quart of champagne apiece, they cast lots, and Dixon won the first rest. And herein, by a decree of that goddess of chance who had watched over them at the casino, ill fortune took good fortune's place upon their trail.

While Dixon snored, Sarding thought of the money in the suitcase, and then he thought of the fact that the secret of the system had been his originally, and that he was entitled to the entire credit for the plan of breaking the bank. Then he meditated upon the circumstance that Dixon, who had done nothing but furnish two-thirds of the capital and play the assistant in the game, would receive a full half of it, and that this was unjust. After a while, he decided that the injustice should be rectified. Why should he not seize the entire winnings and run away with them? A moment's thought showed him that to do this would be both impossible and crude. Then he thought of other plans, and, by and by, he came to the conclusion that the most artistic method of securing Dixon's share of the money would be to win it from him.

Accordingly, next morning, during the latter part of Dixon's first watch, Sarding proposed that they kill time by playing poker. In half an hour, Dixon's share had been reduced to $550. Then, suddenly, Dixon threw down his cards and grabbed those in Sarding's hand. Dixon had two aces, Sarding had three more, and Dixon, without a moment's hesitation, struck him a clean, straight blow between the eyes.

After that, for a minute or two, loud sounds proceeded from the room of the *Americanos*, and there were sundry dull thuds and heavy bumps, and, above all, a loud obligate of yells and profanity. Downstairs, on the veranda of the hotel, the Señor de Vegas was discussing ways and means with the Señor Gonzalez, proprietor of the hostelry, and Count Leon Osterville, and the other señor and the two dons. The Señor Gonzalez left the group and dashed upstairs and into the *Americanos'* room. Dixon was in the act of delivering a second clean, straight blow between Sarding's eyes.

"In ze name of ze law!" exclaimed the Señor Gonzalez, appearing before them.

Dixon and Sarding loosed their fierce embrace and stared at him.

"What do you want?" demanded Dixon.

"I have ze duty to make ze arrest of you," replied the señor smilingly. The Señor de Vegas, the count, the other señor and the two dons appeared in sight behind him.

"For what?" asked Dixon.

"For ze fiendish assault upon ze Señor Sardeeng."

"Away with you," exclaimed Sarding. "*A bas* your law! I refuse to prosecute!"

"Ah," replied Señor Gonzalez, "zen I have ze honair of making ze arrest of ze Señor Sardeeng, also."

"For what?"

"Because he interfere wis ze punishmen' of ze Señor Deexon."

"And who are you?" demanded Dixon, advancing toward the Señor.

"I am ze *maître* of ze hotel," answered the señor, grandly, "and also I am ze prefect of ze police."

A second later, in falling down the stairs backward, the Señor Gonzalez collided with the Señor de Vegas, the Count Leon, the other señor, and the two dons, and after they had picked him up and soothed him, he took counsel with them. Upstairs, in their room, Dixon and Sarding took counsel also, and their first decision was that it would be wise to lock their money in the suitcase and prepare for eventualities.

Ten minutes later, when the Señor Gonzalez returned, accompanied by a file of *rurales,* and ordered them to surrender, they bolted the door and laughed at him. Then, while he made a speech ordering them, upon pain of shooting, to surrender within ten minutes, Dixon noiselessly dropped out of the window in the back of the room to the garden beneath it, and Sarding dropped the treasure to him and followed it. By the time their absence was discovered, Messrs. Dixon and Sarding were safely fortified in a little adobe coconut warehouse in the middle of a clearing on the hillside behind the hotel and the casino.

Just at this moment, a half-breed rushed around to the front of the hotel and revealed the *Americanos'* whereabouts to the Señor de Vegas, and, without delay, the file of *rurales* proceeded to the coconut warehouse and surrounded it. As the Señor Gonzalez, *maître d'hôtel* and prefect, hove into sight, Messrs. Dixon and Sarding were preparing a rampart of coconuts within the closed doors of the warehouse. As he approached the door and bade them surrender, Dixon fired at him with Sarding's pistol, and the Señor Gonzalez, when the bullet whizzed near his head, ducked and fled.

Then began a siege, and the Señor Gonzalez summoned up his forces, and Dixon and Sarding, within the coconut warehouse, built them a fort and set out to beat off their besiegers. When the latter, after a long speech by the Señor Gonzalez, attempted to rush the fort, Dixon opened fire on them, and one of the most valiant soldiers—to wit, Count Leon Osterville, who appeared in the guise of a sergeant of *rurales*—received a bullet through the lobe of the ear. Howling and scared, he beat a hasty retreat, and his fellow warriors followed him.

Thereupon, seeing that brute force was of no avail, and

being in fear of colliding with a bullet himself, the Señor Gonzalez bethought him of a stratagem. He would combat the *Americanos* with fire. He would smoke them out. He would defeat them, and their defeat would be inglorious.

So, a half-breed was told off to sneak up to the warehouse from the rear and to set up a pile of brushwood against the wall. For ten minutes, he tiptoed back and forth with armfuls of dried banana fans and coconut husks and other tinder-like rubbish. While Dixon and Sarding, within, watched the door of the warehouse nervously, in expectation of another rush, the pile of fuel grew behind them and unknown to them, and suddenly it burst into flame. Then Dixon and Sarding smiled grimly and waited in patience for the rise of the curtain upon the next act. The melodrama was becoming interesting.

Outside, the flames crackled and roared, and the forces of the Señor Gonzalez drew nearer, but Messrs. Dixon and Sarding, as yet, did not fear, for the wall of the warehouse was of adobe, and the roof was of galvanized iron, and so it wouldn't burn, and the smoke that curled through the eaves was inconsiderable. A long while would be required to smoke them out, they thought, and in a long while, many plans could be devised, and many accidents might happen.

And even as they expected, an accident happened, though, in truth, it was hardly an accident, because it was merely a natural consequence, and for many days afterward they blamed themselves for having overlooked it. Science, they knew, but forgot, teaches (a) that a coconut is three-fourths water, and (b) that its shell is air-tight. Science, they also knew and forgot, but soon had cause to remember, also teaches that when the water within an air-tight shell is heated to a certain point, it becomes steam, and that, pretty soon, the steam bursts the shell, and there is trouble.

This is what happened in the case of the pile of coconuts beside the rear wall. The fire without heated the adobe, and it became as warm as the bricks in an oven. Then it, in turn, heated the coconuts, and, suddenly, two of the latter exploded, and Messrs. Dixon and Sarding ducked. Thereafter, a dozen exploded in concert, and in a few minutes the interior of the warehouse was much like the interior of a bombarded fort. A large half-section of shell struck Dixon full in the back and floored him, and another shell, a second later, grazed Sarding's head. Then a large and simultaneous explosion of a half-hundred of them cracked the adobe wall, and soon there was a big hole in the wall and the smoke began to pour through it.

Ten seconds later by the clock, Messrs. Dixon and Sarding staggered out of the warehouse by the front door, half suffocated and badly bruised, and the forces of the Señor Gonzalez closed in upon them and captured them and bound them and tore the heavy suitcase from Dixon's weak grasp. Behind them, in the warehouse, lay Sarding's pistol. The Señor Gonzalez laughed loudly. His stratagem had succeeded.

Messrs. Dixon and Sarding, very naturally, were less pleased, and when, after a long march down the hill, they were led to the San Mateo *cuarçel* and locked up together in the only cell, their anger was fearful to behold. When the smoke had left their lungs and their senses returned, they dispatched their guard for their jailer.

In half an hour, the Señor Gastos y Bianca, governor of the city of Tampico, appeared before him. He had shed his frock coat and glossy hat and wore a pair of khaki trousers much too short for him and the upper half of a pair of pink pajamas.

"We want the boss of the ranch," said Sarding.

"I have ze honair," replied the señor, "to be ze prefect to ze *cuarçel*."

"The job, I suppose, is a sideline?" said Dixon sarcastically.

"Si, señor," replied the señor, not comprehending.

"What are we locked up for?" asked Dixon. "As American citizens, we demand to hear the charges against us."

"Ze accusations," replied the señor, "ees, primo, ze endeavor to make ze murdair of ze one anuzzer; secondo, ze endeavor to shoot ze Señor Gonzalez, ze prefect of ze polis; zen comes señor"

"Shooting the Count Osterville?"

"Ze captain of ze port."

"And carrying concealed weapons?"

"Si, señor."

"And interfering with the police?"

"Si, señor."

"And obstructing the free passage of persons passing by and along a public highway?"

"Of zat, I know nozzing."

"And what else?"

"And ze arson of ze house of ze cocoanuts, and ze—"

Sarding reached through the bars of the cell and grabbed the astonished señor's beard, and the señor, with a quick jump and a scream, departed.

"'No hope, no change,'" said Dixon, quoting Kipling, "'the clouds have shut us in.'"

"But we'll bust loose again," replied Sarding optimistically. "Hello, there!"

The guard came running, but stopped beyond reach.

"Summon the American consul," said Sarding.

"Si, señor," replied the guard, and then he set off upon his mission, and Sarding and Dixon waited for his return.

THEY WAITED, in all, four days and four nights, and while they waited, they sweated and stewed and swore. Truly, it was not the season in San Mateo. The weather was not bearable. Up at the hotel upon the hill, in all probability, it was as hot as upon the Niger. Down near the sea, in the *cuarçel,* it was hot beyond human imagination.

Dixon and Sarding stripped to the waist and took turns standing at the little barred window which opened into the overgrown garden behind the tumble-down building, and when they were not thus engaged, they alternately experimented with schemes of escape and gave voice to loud and profane calls for help. The foul air of their cell, and the dreary, enervating heat sickened them, and their state of mind subtracted little from their woe. Where was their money? Where was the suitcase and where were the three thousand, four hundred and fifty dollars? The steamer for Kingston would leave next morning, and here they were in a cell with no chance of release—for the bars were stout and close together—and all their winnings—all the fruit of their industry and ingenuity and craft—commandeered, hypothecated, stolen. In his coat pocket, Dixon had a bank-note for $100. This represented their entire capital.

But, after all, it was well to be patient and to wait for the arrival of the American consul, if the Mexicans would be foolish enough—which now seemed almost unlikely—to summon him. They would offer him a third interest in their claim in return for his private and official aid, and the next act of the drama would be an exciting one—for the Mexicans.

Three times a day, the guard's wife, a dirty, slovenly, half-breed woman, brought them their food—fried plantains, tough chicken hash flavored with garlic, and leathery beef. Each time she called, they inquired for her husband, who was evidently making a search for the consul. But from her they obtained no news, for she spoke neither English nor Spanish, nor, yet, even good Mexican-Spanish, and so they waited and waited and sweated and fumed and swore.

On the evening of the fourth day, the guard returned and announced that the American consul had at last consented to visit them. Five minutes later, the consul appeared. He was the Señor de Vegas, managing director of the San Mateo Casino.

"Ze señors ees surprise," he observed, humorously.

Messrs. Dixon and Sarding were mute.

"Nevairzeless," continued the Señor de Vegas, "I have ze honair to represent ze—what you say—ze Oncle Sam—ees it not? I have ze *Americano* naturalization paper from ze New Olean. Eet ees goot to haf eet eef someone make ze endeavor to—what you say?—bleed me. One *Americano* steamsheep comes here in ze year. I have ze honair to visé hees manifest. I have ze salary of ze one hoondart dollar ze year."

"We demand that you secure our release," said Sarding.

"Ah," replied the señor.

"We demand that our money be returned," said Dixon, "and if you refuse, we'll come back with a warship and blow your ratty casino a mile high—with you in it."

The Señor de Vegas smiled.

"To coom back," he said, "we moos' fairst get avay, is it not?"

The eyes of Dixon and Sarding met, and, simultaneously, they mopped their brows.

"Well, then," said Sarding wearily, "what's your game?"

"I am ze consul," replied the señor slowly. "I have ze honair to be compatriots wis you. But also I am ze director of ze casino. You haf had ze honair of making ze casino go to ze dead broke. I have had ze honair of taking care of ze money zat you win. Eees eet not ze duty of ze *Americano* consul to take care of ze money of ze *Americanos* in ze *cuarçel?* Once more, I am ze director of ze casino. Also I am ze—what you say?—ze—shudge—ze shudge of ze tribunal of ze joostice."

"Pooh, bah!" said Dixon.

"As ze consul," continued the señor, without halting, "I have ze honair to take care of ze money. As ze director of ze casino I have ze honair to haf you arrest for ze swindling of me."

"It was a fair game," said Sarding doggedly.

"As ze shudge," the señor went on, "I haf ze honair of holding ze — what's hees name? — ze inquest on you. Eet will be my shudgment zat you pay me half of ze money back for swindling, and half of ze money for ze punishment for making ze endeavor to shoot ze Señor Gonzalez. *Sabe*?"

NEXT MORNING, Messrs. Dixon and Sarding stood in the bow of the Danish tramp steamer *Bjornmer* as she slowly steamed over the shoal at the entrance of San Mateo harbor and headed east by southeast for Kingston. The captain told them that the Señor de Vegas, the able judge of the court at San Mateo, and the efficient representative of Uncle Sam, had arranged for their tickets. This made the $100 banknote in Dixon's pocket clear capital. He drew it forth, and the two gazed at it.

"We'll begin all over again," said Dixon. "I know of a joint in Venezuela that—"

"We?" said Sarding, and then paused a moment. "Will you shake hands and forget it?" he asked, eagerly. "If I hadn't tried to beat you out of your share, we might have—"

"Aw, forgit it!" said Dixon, lighting a cigarette. "As Kipling says, 'let us leave the dead behind us.' It's over now. Let it rest."

"And we've learned," said Sarding, "that in unity there's strength. In the future, I, for one, shan't forget it."

"Nor I," said Dixon.

And they shook hands.

THE HEATHEN RAGE

MAJOR JOHANN GERST VON BRAUN made his start in life as body servant to an officer in the Hessian army, and with not a sign of a "von" to his name, but the times being favorable to the prosperity of men of his trade, he reappeared before long as a deputy sub-lieutenant or something of the sort and his erstwhile master's social equal, and soon after, for valiant services in the Low Countries, he was given his company.

Then came the difficulty between the King of England and his subjects in America, and Captain von Braun was made a major in a regiment of Hessian grenadiers and sold by his sovereign to the unfortunate George.

Overseas, in a snail-like troopship, he journeyed with his companions, and on a certain memorable day in mid-winter, he and they had the honor of being badly worsted in a battle at a place called Trenton by a general named Washington. Major von Braun himself was wounded in the leg during this action, and a couple of years later, still limping, he applied to the powers that were in those days for a reward for his pain and valor. In the due course of time, this application reached the proper authorities in England, and the West Indian colonies being then anemic for lack of white men, it was deemed expedient to satisfy Braun and aid the colonies at one stroke by making him a colonist.

So, like scores of others of his craft and services, he was informed that the King of England, in the goodness of his royal heart, had determined to make him a present of a princely plantation in the island of Jamaica. There were two thousand acres in this plantation. Ten of them on the top of a mountain were fairly horizontal, and others, on the mountain's upper edges and eaves, were more or less perpendicular. But Major von Braun was not dissatisfied, for he was becoming old and the wound in his leg had destroyed his usefulness as a soldier, and so he sailed for Jamaica and settled on his estate, with a couple of old comrades-in-arms as next-door neighbors, and there, in the course of time, he died, leaving a Jamaican widow of exceedingly dark complexion and a half a dozen Hessian-Jamaican children.

II

ALL OF this is the prologue to the story, and as in a good many other historical dramas—for the matters herein set forth concern the affairs of nations, which are the foundation stones of history—there is a wide stretch of time between the prologue and the other scenes, and a complete change of characters.

Major Braun died and was forgotten, his sons and his sons' sons were married and died and were forgotten, and the various branches of the family returned nearer and nearer to the maternal dark brown. A dense jungle overgrew the estate on the mountaintop, and it was deserted and forgotten, too. That is to say, it was forgotten for more than a century and a quarter. There is a doubt that it ever would have been recalled at all had it not been for the appearance of Mr. Hugo Krause. Mr. Krause, like the forgotten Major Braun, was a gentleman of German birth. Some time before, he had received a polite invitation to depart from the republic of Salvador, in Central America. He had come to Salvador followed by a mulatto official of the Bolivian secret service and had made himself obnoxious by taking a hand in an unofficial lottery scheme.

He left San Salvador in the middle of the night on the tramp steamer *Toltec* and landed at Kingston, with a comfortable shot-bag full of silver and gold. After spending a week in the company of an old friend—an agent for an

American arms company—he went up country to Spanish Town, the ancient capital, for a long rest.

Spanish Town is no longer a town, in the real meaning of the word. It is merely a collection of penitentiaries and traditions. The great white walls of St. Catharine's Prison enclose half of it. The old courthouse across the plaza and the Rio Cobre Hotel, on the banks of the stream beyond, are the only buildings that unfelonious visitors ever enter.

Mr. Krause arrived in Spanish Town in the middle of summer, and in the course of his ride from the little depot to the Rio Cobre Hotel, he saw but one person. Spanish Town was fast asleep, and for a couple of days Mr. Krause spent most of his time imitating it. Then, for want of a better pastime, he began to browse about the old courthouse, with its time-stained records of Spanish and early English rule. The black clerk in charge of the building told him that he might read the old folios and great yellow tomes for the sum of a shilling an hour, cash in advance, and Mr. Krause, having nothing better to do, invested half a crown and drew up his chair.

For a while, he drifted aimlessly through a quaint account of the famous Port Royal earthquake and of the fire of 1816. Then, passing on to less human documents, he dipped into a couple of volumes of ancient deeds and patents. There were records of grants to dukes, barons, viscounts, and commoners; to soldiers, sailors, and men of trade; to British subjects and to allies of the British Crown. In a big, dog-eared book, on the cover of which "Liber" was followed by an unintelligible mark, Mr. Krause found the name of the late and forgotten Major Gerst von Braun.

He was attracted to it because there were Brauns on his own family tree and because the land granted the forgotten major was described with unusual eloquence. To him, said the old patent, and to his heirs and assigns forever, was given "all that lot or parcel of ground lying at and on the mountain or hill called St. Matthew's Peak, and bounded on the north by a line there fixed from the juncture of the stream or water course called Colan's River and the stream or water course called the Rill and running and extending to the landmark set and fixed — "

Mr. Krause closed the book and took a stroll up the road to the Rio Cobre Hotel — now deserted and as quiet as the tomb — and back through the woods to the Rio Cobre itself. He stretched out in the short guinea grass by the bank, in the shade of an old tree, and gazed lazily at the red-beaked John crows circling about against the background of clear blue sky above. He wondered what had become of Major Gerst von Braun and his neighbors of long ago. Times had changed since then, but Jamaica, in Major Braun's day, must have been the same island of delight. The palms were the same, the sky was the same, the long, dreamy days were the same. The old major must have enjoyed the years of his retirement — up there in the mountains, in the rose garden of the earth, with nothing to do but sit in the shade and gaze at the sky and the John crows, and smoke his long Hessian pipe.

Mr. Krause fell asleep after these meditations began to grow wavering, and, in all probability, Major Braun and his grant of land would have passed out of his mind to return no more had it not been that the next week found him profoundly bored. Spanish Town, in summer, was a lotus-eater's paradise, but he, Krause, was scarcely a lotus-eater. The watchword of his life had been action, and the fact that he was in funds and an exile on British soil could not make him forget the joys of having a definite task before him and of harboring a desire to perform it.

For ten years, he had been what his American friends denominated a hustler. Three times, in fact, his energy had passed the bounds set down by the statutes of as many republics. Now, despite the fact that the British laws protected him and there was a credit of more than a thousand pounds in his name at the Colonial Bank, he yearned for something to do.

Consequently, he smiled with great delight when the chief clerk of the German consulate in Kingston, whom he met in the garden of the Myrtle Bank Hotel, invited him to go on an exploring trip into the Blue Mountains. The chief clerk, whose name was Schmidt, was writing a book on the ancient maroon towns, and he desired to visit some of them. Two days later, he and Krause set forth with a train of pack mules and food and drink enough to last a month.

Schmidt's book, *The State of Domestic Architecture and Family Government Among the Aborigine Inhabitants of the British West Indies* (Grosman: Leipzig, 2 vol. folio) contains a minute account of his scientific investigations, and therein also is an elaborate diary of the expedition. But no line of it, except one paragraph, has a bearing upon the history of Mr. Hugo Krause. This one paragraph, translated from the original German (it may be found on page 345 of volume one), is as follows:

August 24 — Camped on crest of eminence called St. Matthew's Peak or Braun's Crest, and there ate the last of our American caviar. K. displayed curious interest when the second (and more common) name of the crest was mentioned, and inquired if Colan's River was near by. On being informed that it was, he made a rough survey of the neighborhood. This amused and puzzled me for some time, but since then—clever rogue!—I have discovered why he was so interested.

III

IT WAS an exceedingly wise old gentleman who said

that the devil finds work for the idle. Mr. Krause, having a thousand pounds in banks and no need to labor, was idle. The fruit of his idleness, in the language of a Kingston paper, was a nefarious "plot." His partner and first victim in the plot was a Jamaican youth of mahogany complexion named James Brown, whom he had employed in the capacity of valet and confidential secretary.

It didn't occur to Mr. Krause at first that Brown might be one of the dead and forgotten Major Braun's heirs.

His first thought, in truth, was that the Braun tract would make a capital coffee plantation and that he (Krause) should be able to buy it for next to nothing. According to the statutes made and provided in Jamaica, abandoned lands revert, in the course of time, to the Crown, and the latter, after seven years of possession, is authorized to sell them to the highest bidder. Mr. Krause thought of making a bid for the Braun estate, which, in default of owners appearing, had probably reverted long ago; but, upon investigating the matter, he found that coffee would not grow on land set at an angle greater than 45 degrees, and that the temperature at the top of the mountain (where he planned to build his home), was uncomfortably low.

Then it was that he thought of the aforesaid James Brown, who, at the moment the thought struck him, was rubbing him down with alcohol as a guard against fever.

"Did you ever know, James," he said suddenly, "that you were a German?"

In Jamaica, it is no disgrace to be a German, and James grinned.

"I never knowed it for sartain," he answered hesitatingly.

"Did you ever know that you were an heir to a big estate?" continued Mr. Krause.

Brown's eyes bulged.

"Me?" he exclaimed.

"Yes," said Mr. Krause, "you."

"Not for sartain," replied the diplomatic Brown.

And then Mr. Krause told him the story—or as much of it as it was well for him to know. The forgotten Major Braun had left between three and ten children. The exact number was unknown, but for the sake of argument, it might be taken as six. Supposing that all these children were sons, that each married and had an equal number of offspring, and that this geometrical progression continued for a century and a quarter—taking all of these things for granted, it would be easy to prove the interest of James Brown in the Braun estate, and easy, also, to explain the hitherto inexplicable preponderance of Browns in the Jamaican population. Every third black Jamaican is named Brown. As a rule, his Christian name is John. The old major's name was Johann Braun, or, in English, John Brown. *Quod erat demonstrandum.*

This reasoning may fall before cold and critical analysis, but in the tropics, where the sun warms the blood, cold and critical analysis is rare. James Brown, the heir of Major Brown, told his brother George Brown, his uncle John Brown, his cousin John Brown and his brother-in-law John Brown. Thereupon, there was excitement in the tribe of Brown. John Browns came from every point of the compass—from Morant Bay, from Spanish Town, from Half-Way Tree, from Salt Pond, from Stony Hill, from every town and village within a day's walk. They came to inquire into the matter, to trace their family trees and to consult Mr. Krause.

Before long, they began to troop in from the mountains—short, knobby-boned, mule-driving Browns from the up-country banana plantations; small householder Browns from the swamps down Old Harbor-way; tall, Diana-like *porteuse* she-Browns from New Castle and Guava

Ridge; ignorant, half-savage Browns from Nanny Town and the depths of the Blue Mountains. They crowded the night shelter in Orange Street and the darky lodging houses and overflowed into the parade. James Brown, valet to Mr. Krause, was appointed grand marshal of these bucolic Browns. He marshaled them in line and made hazy explanations to them, and they gaped and stared and wanted to know when they would get their rights. The yearning of the American ex-slaves for forty acres and a mule was as nothing to the great desire of these Jamaican Browns to take up their residence on their paternal acres and lead lives of carefree content. Their squatting days were over. No longer would harassing landowners force them to move on. Henceforth, they would be landowners themselves.

The day after the beginning of the march of the Browns, Mr. Krause inserted in the *Kingston Daily Gleaner* and the *Kingston Telegraph* the following advertisement:

CLAIMANTS WANTED

Heirs and descendants of the late Major Johann (or John) Braun (or Brown) are respectfully requested to communicate with the undersigned, who is in possession of information to their advantage. All applicants must be prepared to prove their claims for a share of the deceased's vast estate.

A remittance of one shilling should accompany each communication to cover the necessary clerical expenses.

Hugo Krause,
The Myrtle Bank Hotel

This advertisement, if the truth must be told, was a sort

of bait. Mr. Krause wanted to test the temper of the Browns, to sound the depths of their financial responsibility and of their willingness to part with their hard-earned currency. Much beating about the world had taught him that the average man, being given his choice, would take a glittering generality in preference to a cold certainty. The Browns furnished a new proof of it. They took the glittering generality—and they surrendered their greasy shillings.

On the second day of the advertisement's appearance, the manager of the Myrtle Bank Hotel loudly remonstrated with Mr. Krause.

"You're ruining my business," he exclaimed. "You're crowding the courtyard with niggers."

"Why don't you drive them out?" replied Mr. Krause.

The manager glanced out of the reading-room window helplessly. There were a hundred darkies in the palm-shaded courtyard—Browns from the east, Browns from the west, Browns from the north, and Browns from the south. Mr. Krause's confidential valet, James Brown, was passing among them, collecting their shillings and recording their names in a book. It was the beginning of what was destined to go down into history as the rising of the Browns.

IV

THE VARIOUS intermediate causes and reasons which led to the migration and concentration of the Browns of eastern Jamaica might be of interest if this chronicle were planned as a philosophical history like that the late Mr. Carlyle wrote of the French Revolution. But it is not, and so there is need only to record the fact that, after Mr. Krause had obtained the names and shillings of a thousand yellow, brown, yellow-brown, and coal-black Browns, he issued, through his confidential valet, James Brown, a secret order requiring them to repair to the estate of the lamented and once-forgotten Major Johann Braun.

As has been indicated, this estate was in the mountains — in the high, purple, glorious mountains on the north side of the island, from the crests of which, on clear days, it was impossible to see the tips of the dim gray hills of Cuba. It was in these mountains that there occurred the rebellion told of in another place, which little Hurra Lal, the coolie boy, suppressed before it was too late. Far down the slope to the northwest, one might see the glint of the red-tiled roofs of Port Antonio. Nestling in the palms due north, but beyond the shimmering green-blue water of the Caribbean, sat Santiago, behind her hills. It was a safe and snug retreat, and years ago, in the days when brute force reigned, it was a favorite haunt of maroons and — said some authorities — of pirates. But this was long, long ago — before even Major Johann Gerst von Braun appeared. For years now, it had been the abode of peace — of peace and the children of peace — lazy red-gilled John crows, tropical birds of plumage and all the lesser dwellers of the jungle.

At Mr. Krause's behest, the Browns came trooping to their own from near and far. In Portland, St. Andrew, St. Catherine, and Trelawny, they abandoned their palm and bamboo thatch huts, and, loading their children and household goods upon their donkeys, took up the march. Moving, to a Jamaican, is not as serious a business as it is to a Northerner. Given a decent supply of palm "fans" and bamboos, it takes but twelve hours by the clock to build a Jamaican house. What is gained so easily is abandoned without a tear, and so, when a Jamaican moves, he usually touches a match to his late residence and goes on his way rejoicing.

In this manner, then, the Browns came into their own, a thousand strong. For two days they came trooping up the mountainside, and for two days they sat about in calm and peace and boiled green bananas in castaway meat cans. Mr. Krause, gazing upon them, grew rather uneasy. They seemed too mild, too torpid, too inoffensive. They were content, apparently, with the mere knowledge that they had come into their own. If this was a correct guess, there would be no profit in the affair for Mr. Krause. He was a bird of prey who thrived on trouble. The woes of other people constituted his gain.

All of this shows that, in his dealings with the Browns, he was actuated by a rather dark and mysterious ulterior motive. By great ill-fortune, it nearly happened that this ulterior motive was dealt a body blow. On the third day, the Browns grew restless. Were they to be compelled to wait forever, they asked. When was their land to be distributed? Why was Mr. Krause delaying?

Mr. Krause explained that it was necessary to draw up countless reams of legal documents, and showed the delegation that called upon him a stack of "deeds" a foot or more in height. Upon these, he said, he was at work. So the Browns returned to their brethren and the whole family resumed its daily routine of eating bananas and drinking the juice of water nuts, while Mr. Krause sat in his tent on the mountaintop and waited.

This custom of eating boiled bananas, in fact, was the instrument of Mr. Krause's final deliverance, though he did not follow it himself. On the landward slope of the Brown estate was an immense banana plantation, which, until a few weeks before, had been cultivated by a planter named Captain Hopkins. With the first rising of the Browns, Captain Hopkins' mule drivers and machete wielders, all of whom were of the tribe of Brown, disappeared. The overseer, left alone, journeyed to Kingston, where he fell in with an American acquaintance—an agent for a farm implement firm—and (this being a truthful record of fact, the whole truth may as well be told) grew exceedingly intoxicated.

This, then, left the plantation unprotected, for Captain Hopkins himself was on the broad Atlantic, aboard the steamer *Admiral Farragut,* on his way home from a trip to New York. When he arrived at Kingston and journeyed upcountry to his banana fields, he found them sadly wrecked. The Browns had appropriated them. They were eating the green bananas at the rate of 300 bunches, a day. Also, they were robbing the occasional coconut trees of their water nuts and fronds, the plantains of their fruit, the bread-fruit trees of theirs, the mangoes of theirs, and the oranges about the plantation house of theirs. The Browns were committing what the Jamaican political economists call praedial larceny on a colossal scale. They were holding their "property" by force of numbers and consuming it with haste.

When Captain Hopkins discovered all of these things, he well-nigh suffered a stroke of apoplexy. First of all, he rushed back to Kingston and forcibly revived and reviled his somnolent overseer. Then he dashed up Harbor Street to the office of James Radway Higgins, Esq., his attorney, and demanded to know if there were yet laws in the land. Had he not bought his estate at an auction sale of reverted land, and had he not paid ten shillings an acre for it? Was there no law to protect his property from the depredations of a horde of savages who stripped his trees of bananas and brought down his coconuts with clubs and stones and plucked his half-ripe oranges and mangoes? Where was the constabulary? Where was justice?

Mr. Higgins told him to sit tight and wait, and, next day, the impressively dignified Inspector General of Constabulary more than earned the per diem portion of his £850 a year. Mr. Higgins was a K.C. and a man of consequence in the community, and the jolt he administered to the Inspector General, in the name of his client, was an exceedingly severe one. Captain Hopkins, he said, had been outraged.

His property had been seized and destroyed, and not an official voice had cried "halt," nor an official hand moved to protect him. It was a scandal and an outrage, and someone—he would not name the person—would suffer for it. If justice was not to be had in the island, there was the colonial office at home, with Mr. Higgins' brother-in-law sitting on a stool and ready to give ear unto his relative's complaints. The Inspector General, who had planned to attend a garden party that night at King's House, arrayed himself instead in his campaigning togs, and, with two first-class inspectors, three second-class inspectors, and four sergeants-major, set out just as the sun went down for the scene of the disturbance.

The Inspector General traveled all night along the East Coast Road and at sunrise reached Morant Bay. Then he headed northward, and, after lunching at Bath, struck into the John Crow Mountains. When he reached the stronghold of the Browns, it was late in the afternoon, and Mr. Krause very affably invited him to dinner.

"Are you in command of this rabble?" demanded the Inspector General, gazing about him upon five thousand squatting Browns. Most of them had little fires before them, and over the fires they held battered tin cans in which spluttered boiling green bananas. Captain Hopkins, gazing toward his stripped banana trees down the mountainside, grew purple with suppressed rage.

"As I have told Captain Hopkins," replied Mr. Krause, "my sole connection with these people is in the capacity of agent. I am their superintendent."

"But what are they doing here?" demanded the Inspector General.

"And what do they mean by trespassing on my property?" demanded Captain Hopkins.

"The question of the title of the property is one for the courts to decide," said Mr. Krause. "There seems to be a difference of opinion. You claim it as yours, and they think that it is theirs. They are as much entitled to their opinion as you are to yours."

This remark so disconcerted Captain Hopkins that he precipitately retired, and, thereafter, Mr. Krause and the Inspector General held a long conference. At moonrise, when the Inspector General stumbled down the mountain-side to the bed that had been prepared for him in the bachelor's hall of Captain Hopkins', six things had been decided. They were as follows:

(a) Mr. Krause would advise his "clients" to hold their "property."

(b) They would attempt to prove their title to the land in the courts and would resist the legality of its sale, without their knowledge, to Captain Hopkins.

(c) The Inspector General would give them five days to vacate.

(d) If they were not gone by then, a company of constables, or, if need be, of soldiers, would come up from Kingston and push them off the estate at the point of the bayonet.

(e) If they resisted, they would be shot.

(f) If they didn't resist, they would be arrested.

Mr. Krause went to sleep that night smiling a smile of supreme content and righteousness. Trouble was at hand, and ever since trouble had brought about his sudden departure from his fatherland, it had been his friend. Trouble, to him, meant profit.

Here, again, it may be well to pass over some of the happenings in the camp of the Browns. When Mr. Krause informed them in the morning of the Inspector General's ultimatum, they cheered him (Mr. Krause, of course), and told him that they would follow him halfway to Hades. He stood upon a huge flat boulder, and in the early sunlight addressed them. They sat about him on the ground—

Browns, Browns, Browns and Browns. Now and then, they yelled "'Ear! 'Ear!" and "Hurray!" Their wives and their children, their sisters and their aunts, sat with them, and yelled, too.

"They want to rob us!" shouted Mr. Krause. "They want to drive us away—to take our property, to kill us. Will we submit?"

"No! No!" shrieked the Browns.

"Will we resist?"

Some of the Browns did not quite understand the word, but, led by others who did, all bawled, "Yes."

"Then what do we need?" demanded Mr. Krause.

The Browns didn't know.

"What do we need?" repeated the leader.

"Guns!" answered his satellite, the confidential secretary Brown.

"And what must we have to get the guns?" asked Mr. Krause.

"Money!" answered the same gentleman.

"Money!" repeated the others.

Then Mr. Krause explained the thing in detail. It was the privilege of a British subject, guaranteed by Magna Carta, to resist the unlawful and illegal seizure of his property. The law permitted him to shoot. It was his duty to shoot. But, to shoot, he must first secure a gun, and to get a gun, he must first produce money.

There were four hundred Browns capable of bearing arms—a sufficient number, were all well-equipped, to vanquish the whole force of constabulary and militia in the island. Some of the Browns wondered how this could be when it was a notorious fact that the West Indian Regiment alone had a thousand men. But Mr. Krause knew and it was useless to inquire. He was their Moses, and they would follow him out of the wilderness and into the promised land.

Mr. Krause said that he knew a Spaniard in Santiago who had four hundred rifles stolen from the American arsenal, which he would sell for ten shillings apiece. This would mean a bill of four hundred shillings or £200 sterling. Divided among, say, four hundred Browns, it would mean ten shillings apiece. Could that sum be realized?

There were many murmurs when Mr. Krause's harangue reached this stage, and some of the Browns thought the thing rather impossible. In Jamaica, mule-driving (and mule-driving was the ancient and honorable profession of most of the Browns) yielded one an income of but two shillings a day. Ten shillings meant five days' wages. Could the average Brown raise that much? Did he have it with him?

Mr. Krause stepped down from his boulder and ate breakfast, and while he ate, the Browns conferred. Most of them swore to the others they had no money. How could a poor man raise ten shillings? It was wealth. But, after a while, a couple of strong men arose who knew and dared to speak. One of them was John Brown XVIII, who, in his day, had been head waiter at the Titchfield Hotel, at Port Antonio. He would have no shilly-shallying.

"Them thet don't hailp to pay for the guns," he said, "hought to be hexpelled."

Ten other Browns with money agreed with him, and, before long, his sentiment was the sentiment of the majority. And then the minted coin began to roll in. Those Browns who were really penniless borrowed greasy shillings and pennies and "quatties" from those who had a surplus. In blocks of ten shillings, the subscriptions to the stock of the great Brown Defense Syndicate, Unlimited, began to roll in. They rolled in toward evening and Brown, the confidential secretary of Mr. Krause, entered the names of all the subscribing Browns in a big book. Mr. Krause placed the money—when all had stepped up, the amount was rather more than £350 — in three shot bags and sealed them with a candle. Then he explained his plan.

"Tonight," he said, "I'll go down to Lynch's Bay and hire a schooner. With Mr. Brown here" — indicating the confidential secretary — "I'll set sail for Santiago. The round trip, if the wind is favorable, ought to take three days. In Santiago, I'll buy the four hundred guns and get them back here by Thursday morning. I'll land them opposite the little island that Mr. Brown says stands out in Fairy Hill Bay, and you men be there — say fifty of you — to meet me. We'll get the guns and the ammunition — I'm going to pay for the ammunition out of my own pocket" — cheers and cries of "'Ear, 'ear" — "we'll get the stuff here, I say, before the constables arrive. And then we will give them a reception that'll teach them not to interfere with honest men's rights."

The Browns thought this a delightful plan, and that night, when Mr. Krause and his friend Brown left the camp, the whole thousand turned out to bid them Godspeed. As Mr. Krause had said, he journeyed down the mountain toward the sea. Toward dawn, he reached St. Mark's, with Brown following behind him, painfully transporting the shot bags of money. By the time the sun was well up, the pair reached the glassy green little inlet called Fairy Hill Bay, and there, awaiting them, was one of the clumsy little schooners with which the black Jamaicans transact their legal and *sub rosa* business with Cuba.

Brown's brother-in-law was asleep in the stern, and he continued to sleep during the greater part of the trip up the coast. For some unknown reason, Mr. Krause directed that the course be made not toward Santiago, in Cuba, but toward Port Antonio, in Jamaica. Port Antonio, in consequence, was reached that afternoon, and Mr. Krause and Mr. Brown, accompanied by shot bags, embarked upon the steamer *Leon* for Boston.

For five days and for five nights, the Browns on the mountaintop waited and waited and waited. Then there came a company of constables who beat the Browns into line and marched them off to Port Antonio, two by two, and handcuffed.

Mr. Krause, at the time, was seated upon the deck of the *Leon,* smoking a cigar and watching the lights of Boston harbor loom into view ahead. He was wondering if any brash detective would remember him as the man for whose arrest the Brazilian minister at Washington had offered a reward.

THE FEAR OF THE SAVAGE

EVERYBODY KNOWS, of course, that magic is out of fashion, and that the last witch was burned at Salem ever so many years ago. This is plain, because it is written in the books, and besides, the left hind foot of a graveyard rabbit is now worth no more in the open market than any other foot of any other animal. Nevertheless, if you were to get a pass entitling you to half an hour's conversation with a certain Benjamin Johnson, a prisoner on the "colored side" of Baltimore City Jail, you might begin to wonder if the wise men really are very wise.

The beginning of this story, however, is not with Benjamin Johnson, but with John Brown. Every black man in the island of Jamaica, in the British West Indies, except forty, or maybe fifty in each hundred, is named Brown. John, being black and a Jamaican, and a son of Henry of that ilk, took the name like the others. Perhaps it appeals to some hidden chord in the African-Jamaican inner consciousness; more likely, it is popular because it is sonorous and easy to spell.

In theory, Henry, the father of John Brown, was a driver of mules at the Misty Valley banana plantation, which is on the north coast of the island, near Port Antonio. This theory was a true one from seven o'clock each morning, except Saturdays, until four o'clock each afternoon. Before and after these hours, and between eleven o'clock and noon—which is ordinarily occupied by banana plantation mule drivers in eating what they call breakfast—he was an *obeah* man, which means a preacher and physician to whom the hymn book and pharmacopoeia are useless—a lawyer, a judge, civil, criminal and ecclesiastic; a tax collector, a protector of the poor and a worker of spells. When his medical patients are ill, the *obeah* man works spells to cure them. When his legal clients have grievances, he works spells to give them their rights. When his other patrons—religious or secular—are in trouble, he works spells to get them out of it. Also, when he is in need of food or clothing, or lodging or money, he works spells to obtain it.

Such a man was Henry Brown, driver of mules. His son, John, at the age of fifteen, became a roustabout, or stevedore, in the employ of the Banana Trust. Every Monday morning, with forty-nine fellow-workers, he reported to the superintendent at the Port Antonio warehouse. Then he lay about in the shade and watched the red-beaked John crows circling about in the blue overhead until a steamer siren tooted beyond the round little island which keeps the Caribbean rollers out of the placid little harbor. When the empty steamer tied up at the dock, he boarded her, in company with his forty-nine companions, and went to sleep again beneath her forward awning. At each out-port, he awoke and helped to pass to the hold the bananas brought from the shore by the surf-boat men. When the hold was full, he went to sleep once more, and did not awake again until the steamer was off the Port Antonio Harbor and the wide, flat surf-boats came out to take her crew of roustabouts ashore. Thus John, the son of Henry Brown, passed his time—sleeping, loading bananas and sleeping again—and, incidentally, he learned from his father, the *obeah* man, many queer things not set down in books.

One day, he went aboard the British tramp steamer *Sussex* at Port Antonio and was carried to Buff Bay and Port Maria. At the former place, he was bitten by a large, hairy spider, and at the latter he fell overboard while attempting to lift a ten-hand bunch of bananas from the *Sussex'* forward port platform to her rail. In consequence of the spider's bite and his ducking, he became even more than usually sleepy, and on the return trip to Port Antonio, he sought a sunny place behind a coil of cable. There, he slept peacefully until the sun went down and the sudden tropic night came and the *Sussex* stopped off Folly Point Light to send her men ashore. It was pitch dark when her engines halted and nobody noticed him. When he awoke, the dawn was breaking over the coast of Haiti, and Cape Maysi, Cuba, was dead ahead.

As he rubbed his eyes and staggered to his feet, Captain Thompson, the *Sussex'* commander, stood before him.

"A stowaway!" gasped the captain.

John, in a trembling voice, murmured an apologetic protest.

"You black rascal!" exclaimed the captain.

"Ah ovah-slep' mahself," said John in terror.

"You soot-faced brigand!" bellowed the captain. The mate on the bridge peered down through the dawn mist in alarm.

"Mr. Robinson!" called the captain, and the mate descended to the deck.

"Put this man in chains!" ordered the captain, "and prepare a raft for launching. We'll set him adrift when we get to Maysi."

Whereupon John, the son of Henry Brown, broke down and wept, and for the space of ten minutes groveled on the deck and begged the captain of the *Sussex* to spare him. At half-minute intervals, the captain interrupted him to dilate upon the wickedness of stowaways and to describe, in forceful language, his plans for driving them from the seas.

"I've had enough of it," he said with vigorous gestures. "First, it was that Dago that sneaked aboard at Genoa. When we got to New York, he slid ashore, and I had to pay a five-hundred-dollar fine. Then it was that half-breed Mexican at Tampico. He brought yellow fever with him, and we lay in quarantine for three weeks. Then it was that coon at Jacmel. When I put him to work, the rascal threatened to knife me, by George—threatened to knife me!—

me!"

The captain's voice rose to a scream.

"Ah couldn't hailp it, cap'n!" wailed John piteously.

"Of course not!" replied the captain with heavy sarcasm. "Of course not! Of course not! Neither could I help it if I hanged you to the derrick boom."

At this, John clutched the rail and shrieked with terror, but in truth he had no need to do so, for the captain really intended to neither hang him nor to set him adrift. This was shown ten minutes later, when he was ordered to march aft to the galley and help the cook peel potatoes for dinner.

Then he was set to scouring pans and polishing knives, and later to scrubbing the galley and blacking the stove and renovating the captain's boots. Being a British subject, and by profession a stevedore, he very naturally regarded such tasks as degrading. On the second day, he approached the captain boldly and said so. For an answer, he received a hard, straight blow upon the angle of the jaw. When he came to life again, he was in chains, and, thereafter, he said no more.

On the third day, he was set free and ordered to paint the forward donkey engine. He added another eighth of an inch to its gummy red coating without a word. Then he was told off to help one of the coal-passers at the ash hoist. It was hard work, and in the hot sun, with the *Sussex* rolling like a water-logged scow and the biting salt spray dashing into his face, he was exceedingly uncomfortable; but experience had taught him prudence, if not contentment, and so he remained silent and worked industriously. After the same manner, for the balance of the voyage, he was a model of diligence. By the time the Chesapeake capes were reached, Captain Thompson almost felt kindly toward him.

But, after the pilot had climbed over the side and the low Virginia shore was to starboard and port, the *Sussex* commander thought it only a sensible precaution to give his unwelcome passenger a solemn and terrifying lecture.

"You are a criminal," he said with a fierce frown. "A felon, by George, and an offense against God and man. At the present moment, you are within the boundaries of the United States of America, where they hang stowaways from the yard-arm. In consideration of your youth, I'm goin' to spare you—in this case. But remember"—and the captain's voice rose to a roar—"if you try to sneak ashore when we get to Baltimore, I'll put the law on you!"

John, very plainly, was properly impressed, and might have been permitted to roam at large over the ship with perfect safety; but when the *Sussex* entered the Patapsco and tied up at her berth at Bowley's wharf, and the custom-house officers demanded that the captain fill and sign a large printed form giving detailed information about his unwelcome passenger and suitable guarantees that the latter would not go ashore, his anger against the luckless John returned, and, late in the afternoon, after a cargo of bananas had been discharged, he ordered John to leave the forecastle and to go on deck.

At dusk, the captain arrayed himself in his most presentable uniform, lighted a genuine three-for-a-shilling Jamaican cigar, and prepared to journey to a certain cafe on Gay Street, where shipmasters congregate and the talk is amusing and congenial, and there are strange and delicious drinks of Maryland nativity and manufacture. As he passed to the ladder, he detected John, who was sitting upon the edge of the forward cargo hatch, in the act of gazing longingly at a fried-fish stall up the wharf toward Pratt Street.

"Aha!" exclaimed the captain, so suddenly that John jumped as if struck, "you're thinking of leaving us. Goin' to jump, eh? You black-hearted, scow-footed, chalk-eyed scoundrel! Mr. Robinson! Mr. Robinson!"—the mate came running—"Put this perjuring murderer in chains. Chain him up to the rail—or to the donkey engine. And set a guard over him—armed."

Red-faced and breathless with rage, the captain disappeared over the side, and as he walked up the wharf, he stopped now and then to gaze back at the terrified John and to shake his fist menacingly. In a moment, the mate came with a heavy leg chain—the same that John had worn for a while during the voyage—and in another moment it was about John's leg, he was lying on the deck beside the forward donkey engine, and a Danish coal-passer was posted before him, armed with an out-of-date trade gun of mammoth bore.

The Dane regarded his prisoner with expressionless eyes and leaned against the rail to rest. All day, since four o'clock in the morning, he had been at work—first at his regular and lawful labor, and secondly at the unpleasant task of renovating the *Sussex'* after-hold. As the dusk came on and silence settled over the ship and the dock, he chewed his quid of natural leaf meditatively and gradually sunk into a half-doze.

Along Pratt Street, but a stone's throw away, trolley cars were banging their way eastward and westward, for it was summer, and thousands of sun-baked Baltimoreans were on their way to the resorts along the river. Now and then, too, a slow-moving policeman stalked down the wharf and gazed idly at the *Sussex*. But, as the evening wore on, the noise of the trolley cars grew less—for the sun-baked Baltimoreans were at their destinations and it was too early for them to return—and the policeman appeared less frequently. Then the Dane with the trade gun fell asleep and soon he was snoring gently, in comfort and in peace.

Meanwhile, John lay upon the deck, resting his head upon his hand and meditating upon his return to his native shores. If this was America, he was sick of it—sick of its cruel customs, its sights, its laws, its people, its noises and its smells. The heavy slime of the sewerage-laden harbor was but a poor substitute for the blue-green of the smiling Caribbean. The dingy brick of the wharf warehouses ill-compared to the splendor of the crotons and the palms. It was a "melancholious country," certainly. The sky was muddy, the landscape was gray, and the people were brutes.

Suddenly, from down the harbor, appeared a crowded excursion steamer, with hundreds of lights along her deck and upon her walking beam, and a tall ray from a giant searchlight flashing round in the sky above her. John gazed at her in wonder, for ships of her kind were new to his eyes, and at last, when she tied up at her slip and her lights began to go out one by one, he wondered why she had so many of them. In Jamaica, the regulations required but three lights—a red, a white, and a green. America, certainly, was a strange country.

Then the man on the deck of the excursion steamer gave the searchlight a few valedictory twirls before shutting it down for the night, and, suddenly, the beam swung around and flashed the length of the *Sussex,* startling John badly. But it did not startle him enough to rob him of the sense of sight, and in its gleam he saw something that caused him to lay as still as the sleeping Dane.

Beside the *Sussex,* in the shadows, a small skiff was slowly moving, and in the skiff was a black man who peered up at the vessel stealthily. John slowly and cautiously wriggled over toward the rail, as far as his chains would permit, and peeped down at the skiff and the black man. In a moment, they disappeared under the stern and then, being trained to listen, John heard the skiff move slowly close to the side until it came amidships. Then John half-closed his eyes and fixed them steadily upon the rail directly above the skiff and the black man.

It was as dark as a cave at that spot, but John, being rather less than a semi-savage, had the senses of a dog, and in a moment he saw two black hands clutch the ridge of metal in which the rail was fixed. Then, between them appeared a black head and two shining eyes which rolled about cautiously and closely scrutinized the deck. After another moment or two, a black form slowly rose from the outer dark and, suddenly, a man sprang noiselessly to the iron plating and slunk into the shadow beside the deck house.

At this, John began to snore gently and to breathe slowly and regularly. The Dane beside him was motionless, and, but for his heavy snoring, might have seemed lifeless. In the shadow, towards the chart-room, the black man crept slowly, with the movements of a wild beast sneaking upon its prey. As he came to the chart-room comer and espied the two men by the donkey engine, he halted and narrowly watched them. Then, satisfied that they were both soundly asleep, he crept towards them and examined them closely. At sight of the gun in the Dane's arms, he drew back a moment and apparently considered the chances of abstracting it. But it was so lying that an attempt to take it might awaken its guardian, and then there might be trouble.

So the black man dropped to the deck and wriggled back, like a snake, towards the chart-room. As he turned, John's eyelids parted just a wee bit and his snore increased in volume. Slowly and painfully, the black man wriggled to the chart-room, and then he reached up and turned the knob of the door and pushed it half open and slipped in.

Thereupon, John, the son of Henry Brown, the *obeah* man, opened his eyes wider and watched the door. For what seemed half an hour, it remained closed. Then it slowly opened, so slowly that an observer might not have guessed it was moving, and as slowly appeared the black man. As he emerged, John's snore rose loudly, and the black man dropped to the deck and began tying up certain things in a bandana handkerchief. There was the captain's second best watch, a small sextant, a meerschaum pipe, a gold matchbox, and a few coins. The black man had difficulty in crowding all into the handkerchief, and as he noiselessly arranged and rearranged the bundle, John's snore mounted higher and higher.

By and by, just as the black man had completed his work and was turning about to creep towards the rail, a new note appeared in the harmony of the snore. It was a queer, minor flat and it seemed to come from the sleeper's throat. The black man stopped suddenly and listened, and the new note changed to a sort of musical trill—and then to an uncanny rattle.

With a crash, the black man dropped the handkerchief and its contents to the deck and halted as if shot. His eyes opened so that the whites gleamed in the half light and his teeth began chattering. Then the rattle became a long roll of sound, with regular rises and falls, and singularly recurring tremoli. At intervals, a deep, low note appeared as from afar, and after it, every time, sounded a faint hiss, like the voice of a snake.

It was the snake-call in the chant of sacrifice, and John, the son of Henry Brown, the *obeah* man, was sounding it as he had heard his father sound it the day that the man who killed the overseer's son on the Misty Valley banana plantation came running out of the jungle and into his captor's arms.

As the first hiss sounded, the black man's face grew gray, and his eyes started from their sockets. Unwilling and helpless, he turned his head towards John, and John's eyes, now open and gleaming, sunk into his soul. Through the poor thing that served for his brain, terrifying pictures were whirling. One picture was a river bank, with tall trees of queer shape all about and the red sun directly overhead. On the bank, a huge fire leaped and crackled, and in the fire were human bones. And there was a man with a knife who sneaked up slowly, and slowly drew the knife—

Suddenly, all of the pictures left the black man's brain and he groveled and squirmed upon the deck in wild, insensate terror—blind terror of the sort that comes to a man through countless generations and beats his education and civilization to the ground with one blow.

To the white man, this terror comes but once or twice in a lifetime—once, maybe, when he is alone in a wood at night, and the forest devils of his ancestors stalk forth to peer at him; and once again, perhaps, when he is alone with the dead. Civilization has been at work upon him long enough to mark him. His fear of the unknown and of the unknowable is covered by his egotism. It is a disgrace to be afraid. But, to the black man, this fear comes often in the night, for his great-grandfather fought his great-granduncle-in-law with poisoned arrows, and the victor ate the vanquished, and so, when the fear of the savage settles upon him, when the snake-call of the *obeah* man sounds, he is a savage once more—a savage upon the banks of the Niger, with the high priest of his tribe advancing towards him, to sacrifice him to the scaly gods of the river.

The snake-call ceased, and in its place rose a shrill bark, like the cry of a wild beast after human prey. With a shriek of insane terror, the black man rose to his knees, and then, as weak and as helpless as a man paralyzed by a blow, he fell forward upon his face and groveled upon the deck, speechless and limp. A queer, half-forgotten sentence in a half-forgotten tongue came from John, the son of the *obeah* man, and the black man groveling on the deck became motionless and rigid.

Then the Dane, who had been startled by the shriek, turned over sleepily and gazed open-mouthed at the captive.

"Take mah chain, 'en chain 'im hup," said John quietly.

"He's stole the capt'in's luggidge."

The Dane obeyed mechanically—for he was trained to obey—and the black man lay still. Then John spoke a word to him and he arose. His eyes still started from their sockets and he was trembling.

"Lemme go!" he whispered, "Foh de good Lawd, lemme go!"

His terror awakened the Dane's sense of humor.

"I shoot you," said the Dane jovially, seizing the trade gun. And he fired over the side into the water, and the police came running, and by the time the captain returned zigzag down the wharf, Benjamin Johnson, colored, was a prisoner at the Central Police Station.

When the captain told the story to the white supercargoes in the Jamaican coast towns, they laughed and said that it was plain; but, though the captain in some way realized that John was to be thanked, and accordingly permitted him to return home as a semi-passenger in the forecastle, he is still much in the dark. This is because there are many things that even a ship captain cannot understand.

THE BEND IN THE TUBE

FIRST OF ALL, Boggs was a lunatic, which was nobody's fault. Secondly, he had a new theory concerning the redemption of silver certificates and the circulation of national banks, which was his own fault. In the third place, he was an anarchist, which was the fault of a good many people, individually and collectively.

All of his acquaintances, from those he casually addressed on the street as "How-are-you" to his blood relatives, had heard him explain his theory of certificates and circulation, and nearly all of them knew that he was a lunatic. The fact was so obvious and patent that it oozed out of every pore of his skin. It was apparent in his clothes, in his conversation, in the mixed drinks that he fancied, and in many other ways. But comparatively few knew that he was an anarchist, and these, being *participes criminis*, said nothing. Schwartz knew and Lowe knew, and so did Zimmerman, and Goldbloom, the Russian, and Kraus, the Austrian. But Murphy, the managing editor of the *Tribune*, was as innocent of the fact as the Grand Lama of Tibet, and equally unknowing and unsuspecting were Gaylor and Smith, who were Boggs' desk neighbors, and Hemming, who was the *Tribune's* business manager. Had these latter been wiser in their generation, they might have saved themselves much trouble.

Boggs, to the outward eye, seemed an eminently harmless sort of crank. Beginning manhood as a divinity student, he had left college under a cloud of heresy, and then, dropping a step further down the scale of brute creation, he had become a reporter on the *Tribune*. Ten years of hard service on the street had been rewarded with the gift of a desk job at $1,200 a year. Now he was financial editor for the *Tribune,* and over five of its columns each morning exercised absolute control—with a reservation, that is, taking account of the superior authority of Murphy, of Murphy's boss, of Murphy's boss's boss, of the boss of Murphy's boss's boss, and, finally, of that awful and mysterious man, the Owner.

In theory, Hemming, the business manager, was not one of these bosses. He was not paid to regulate Boggs' doings—which was the task of Murphy and of the other bosses, in ascending scale—but, as a matter of fact, the business manager of a newspaper, being the man in direct charge of the cash drawer, usually commands much respectful attention, if not affection. Consequently, when Hemming blew a blast into his speaking-tube, and the whistle at Boggs' desk shrieked shrilly, and Hemming's voice from below asked if United States Hardwood 4's had reached 24¾, Boggs usually answered.

Hemming was in the habit of asking questions of this sort at intervals of ten minutes between the hour of one o'clock in the afternoon, when Boggs began work, and that of 3 o'clock, when the stock exchange closed. Boggs, beginning by labeling him a nuisance, ended by regarding him as the living incarnation of all that was iniquitous and depraved. But, as has been mentioned, he was business manager of the *Tribune*, and so Boggs had to answer him, and even to make a show of politeness.

Hemming had begun life with an inheritance of $50,000 in cash, which sum, by judicious speculation, he had reduced to $20,000 in three years. Boggs, knowing this, considered him an ass, which was a just estimate. In addition, he thought him a criminal, which was scarcely logical. Boggs was seldom logical. He knew the exact difference between Sugar and sugar, his head was filled with millions of figures, and he could explain the method of ratiocination whereby the promoters of the Hemp Trust evolved fabulous paper-profits from gigantic factories that did not exist, but his the-

ory of silver certificates and bank circulation bore down upon him heavily, and he believed that all speculation, whether successful or not, was as utterly pernicious as certain of
the theological dogmas that he had rejected years before.

Unlike most financial reporters and editors, he had never risked a dollar on a tip, either "inside" or outside, and
had never entered a broker's office, bucket-shop, or pool-
room except in his capacity of seeker after information for
the great, uncultured public. Many a time he observed
what seemed to be chances to make a safe profit, and sometimes subsequent events showed him that these chances
had been good ones. But he resisted all temptations to
make experiments. For his $1,200 a year, he was content to
edit the exchange and market reports that came to the *Tribune* and to write his daily column of "Jottings in the Street."
In his early massacre of theological principles, he had used
the knife, too, upon the accepted code of ethics, but an in-
junction against coveting the things that are one's neigh-
bor's he had retained.

Thus Boggs lived and had his being, sitting at a desk
seven or eight hours a day, with a scissors and paste-pot
before him, and with a growing dislike of Hemming in his
soul. After his work was done in the evening, it was his
custom, as it is of men whose inward strugglings are less
fatiguing, to seek relaxation. The reaction that followed his
days of yielding to an ascetic faith had sent him bounding
into the purgatory of the unregenerate, and he had made
personal tests of the flavor and virtues of many alcoholic
drinks. After a while, he had concluded that of all on the
cafe card, plain draught beer was at once the most pleasing
and the cheapest. Hunting about for a quiet place to drink
it, he had happened upon Bauermeister's saloon, which
lurked in the dark recesses of an inconspicuous side street,
and in Bauermeister's, by the natural operation of the law
of evolution and opportunity, he had met Schwartz, Lowe,

Zimmerman, and company.

It was a full year before they deigned to wish him a good evening, and after that, he had to buy many a keg of beer, glass by glass, before they invited him into the little back room to which they retired at midnight, when Bauermeister turned out the lights in his bar room and gave his patrons their choice of slinking into dingy apartments in the rear or taking their departure. Schwartz, Lowe, Zimmerman, and company had a private room of their own, for their trade was unfailing and profitable. It was in this room, which badly needed papering and scrubbing, that Boggs first hearkened unto the doctrine that whatever is, shouldn't be.

At first, this rather shocked him, for he had inherited a respect for vested rights from a thousand years of eminently proper ancestors, just as he had inherited his sandy hair and the peculiar curve of his nose. But, after a while, he discovered that many of the things that his new friends told him coincided with his own notions. They believed, for instance, that there was something radically wrong with the American banking system, and they were opposed to laws that made a man do things he didn't want to do. Also, they talked much against the unearned increment, which Boggs soon recognized as merely another way of denouncing thieving, mortgage-owning, grave-robbing, "high-finance"-ing, forgery and speculation—all of which he bracketed together as subdivisions of the same crime.

Thereafter, Boggs began to read the works of the greater radicals, and to evolve theories of his own. Sometimes he grew sadly muddled and had to spend long hours in wakeful meditation, as, for instance, when he tried to reconcile his belief that, in the American national banking system, no rights were allowed the depositor, and his theory that the acceptance of interest on money was ethically indefensible. But Schwartz and Zimmerman showed him a way out of each of these difficulties.

"Vhatefer ain't righdt," said Zimmerman, "out to be ap-polished."

And so Boggs became a sort of wholesale abolitionist, with many strange theories besides that concerning the redemption of silver certificates, and, by and by, he found himself attacking Herbert Spencer because the Spencerian idea regarding the limitation of governmental activity had too many reservations, and criticizing Darwin and Huxley because those best rewarded and protected in human society seemed to him to be least fitted to survive.

Meanwhile, he began work at the *Tribune* office each afternoon at one o'clock and pottered along until 10 or 11 each evening. After that, he journeyed to Bauermeister's to discuss the lamentable state of the world with Schwartz, Kraus, Zimmerman, and the others. Sometimes they palavered until dawn. At other times, they went home after an hour's session, and Boggs shuffled off to his furnished room, to lie awake in the darkness and wrestle with problems that philosophers gave up as insoluble two thousand years before he was born.

One week, Hemming managed, by dumb luck, to make $2,500 by a rise in Union Leather. Thereafter, dropping Copper, B.L.&X., Globe Assurance Incomes, Wire Rope 5's, and other of his old favorites, he made Leather his alpha and omega. There was a ticker beside Boggs' desk—put there more for ornament and to impress visitors to the office than for any useful purpose—and Hemming, coldly perspiring in his office on the ground floor, two flights below, summoned Boggs to the speaking-tube with spasmodic persistence to beg a recital of the tale its rattling told. The speaking-tube system of the *Tribune* office was a relic of the old days of hand-composition and chalk plates, but Hemming preferred it to the telephone, which had strange buzzings to annoy and waits to wait and feminine and world-wise operators to overhear. Boggs groaned each time its shrill whistle sounded.

"How about Leather 39's?" Hemming would ask from below.

"Eighteen and a half," Boggs would answer curtly.

"What do you think—" Hemming would begin, and Boggs would hang up the tube.

Five minutes later, there would come another blast.

"Was that bid or asked?" Hemming would inquire.

"Bid," would be Boggs' reply, and then, for ten or fifteen, or even, when Hemming was enchained by callers, for twenty minutes or half an hour, Boggs would labor away at his flimsy and his market letters.

Once he conceived the idea of ruining Hemming at one stroke by giving him false quotations. He tried the scheme when there came a sudden fall in Leather income 4's. Boggs told him, instead of the truth, that there was a mysterious and steady rise, and said that the bonds had already reached 24, when, as a matter of fact, they were selling at 10. He took some pains with the lie, and volunteered the opinion, which he said was justified by a reliable rumor, that "insiders," with "straight" information, were buying heavily. But either Hemming grew suspicious on account of his willingness to hold converse, or the bucket-shop man to whom the business manager's order was sent by messenger gave him warning, for, apparently, he didn't buy.

Another time, by laying more careful plans, Boggs lured Hemming into buying wheat and had the pleasure of observing him lose $2,000 in eight minutes by the clock. But his allegation that the ticker had made a mistake was denied and disproved, and if good luck hadn't made Hemming win back the money next day by a deal in corn, he might have lost his official head.

Boggs, in time, almost grew resigned to his troubles, for he lived in constant hope that someday Hemming, as he said, would "lose his hide." In three years, he had dropped $30,000, and though his rate of loss had decreased with the growth of superior knowledge, and he was cautious enough to avoid such things as gold-mining schemes and 40 percent Mexican plantation projects, there was still a possibility that, someday, a particularly good "tip" might wipe him out. Boggs believed that no merely mortal man was without his woes, and that no job, office or position was wholly pleasant. Balloonists, he used to say, had an unsurpassed view of the scenery, but there was always a possibility that it might collide with them, and millionaires, though lacking nothing else, seldom had good digestions. So he regarded Hemming as the cross that had been given him to bear and relieved his mind by discussing the Hemming vices and iniquities with his friends, Schwartz, Zimmerman, and company.

But, in time, there comes a straw to break every suffering camel's back, and Boggs' came when Hemming proposed that the *Tribune* subscribe to a Wall Street news service which reported the movements of certain outlawed and degenerate stocks that the ordinary reporting associations did not "cover." This service was designed primarily for afternoon papers, and thereon Boggs based his objections to it. The *Tribune* was a morning paper, and there was no need for it to receive Wall Street news before one or two o'clock, when the morning news associations sent out their first "copy." Besides, there was the ticker, which clicked all day. But Hemming had arguments ready for all of these objections. There were thousands of readers, he said, who were interested in the outlawed stocks, and the morning news associations paid no heed to them. By subscribing to the afternoon service aforesaid, the *Tribune* would attract this large class of readers, and profit much thereby. The plan, said Hemming, commended itself to his business sense and his native intuition.

Boggs suspected that Hemming probably wanted the service for his own information and edification too, but journalistic etiquette stood in the way of saying so. Hemming, finding his arguments weak, dismissed them as of no account, and then laid his plan before Murphy, the managing editor, who, by this same etiquette, had what was ostensibly the deciding voice. Murphy flattered himself that he knew Hemming's real motive as well as Boggs, but life is a series of compromises and he observed an opportunity to make one. He had long wanted the salary allowance of the art department increased by $1,500 a year, and Hemming had long maintained that the *Tribune* could not afford it. Now Hemming diplomatically hinted that he had begun to realize the soundness of Murphy's arguments—and Murphy decided that the extra service would be a good thing. The editor-in-chief and the general manager, who do not enter into this tale, were shadowy figures in the rear, and did not concern themselves with the exchange. It was an affair of outposts.

NOW, IN TRUTH, began the winter of Boggs' discontent. It was a nuisance to plow through the three-score telegraph "flashes" that the outlaw service sent forth every day, and it was a far greater nuisance to tabulate them. When Boggs reached his desk at one o'clock the first day, he found a huge stack of envelopes awaiting him. Soon Hemming fell into the habit of sneaking upstairs in the morning to pry into these messages. Boggs, to whom neatness and order constituted a religion, rebelled against the disarray he encountered on his arrival. So he came to the office earlier and earlier—at 12:30, at noon, and finally at 11 o'clock—cutting short his sleep and morning constitutional and disturbing the charwoman and loafing messenger boys.

Besides, there was the added and tenfold nuisance of increased calls from Hemming in the afternoon. Sometimes he made three inquiries in fifteen minutes, and after a while he fell into the habit of watching the approach of the messenger boys from his office window and of calling up Boggs before they had half climbed upstairs.

He had subscribed to a Jersey City financial journal devoted to booming obscure stocks for cash in hand, and had read therein that the first mortgage bonds of a certain irrigation company in Wyoming were better, as permanent investments, than British consols. Deducing from this that they were sure to soar, he bought a big block of them, and began to read the notices of auction sales of steam yachts. The *Tribune's* new Wall Street service contained frequent mention of these bonds, and Hemming discovered, by close observation, that they were usually offered just before the close of the market each day. In consequence, he fell into the habit of asking Boggs about them half an hour or so earlier, and of repeating his request at intervals of from three to eight minutes.

One day, in disgust, Boggs determined to resign. The limit, he decided, had been reached. His ordinary duties, of course, were pleasant enough, and Murphy and the others, albeit they made fun of his theories and opinions, never bothered him. But the Hemming nuisance he could not bear. He was an editor, and not an office boy, and he would not consent to remain the lackey, actual or in effect, of anyone. He had saved $500, and with this he proposed to make a trip to Europe. On his return, there was little doubt that he could obtain a respectable position on some other paper. His worth, he thought, was known.

On a sheet of yellow copy paper, Boggs wrote his resignation, and after carefully rereading it, inserted it in an envelope addressed to Murphy. Then, of a sudden, he concluded that such a mild-mannered and ladylike leave-taking would not be commensurate with the ills he had suffered. It would be too much like kissing the hand that had smitten him. So he leaned back in his chair and corrugated his brow, and in a little while he had evolved a scheme for a more spectacular departure.

First of all, he would give Hemming a carefully-safeguarded bogus "tip" and make him lose at least $1,000. Secondly, he would walk out of the office at 5 o'clock, with the day's financial copy under his arm, and leave the *Tribune* to scramble for the news later as best it could. Thirdly, he would drop all of the office financial reference books and records of stock variations down the elevator shaft. Fourthly, he would smash the ticker. Fifthly, he would proceed to Hemming's office, downstairs, and favor that gentleman, in profane and insulting language, with his opinion of him.

IT MUST BE remembered (a) that Boggs — from his point of view, at least — had suffered much, and (b) that he was a lunatic. These circumstances, combined, led him to consider his plan of revenge with something akin to the pride of invention and creation. He thought so well of it, in truth, that he could not resist the temptation to unfold it to Schwartz, Zimmerman, Goldbloom, and his other friends at Bauermeister's. He told them that he would soon say *au revoir* and set off for Europe, and that he proposed to depart in a blaze of red fire.

"Vhy don't you knock de tam fool's head off?" asked Kraus.

"Sure," said Zimmerman, "vhy not strike a blow?"

"How?" asked Boggs.

The others laughed in chorus.

"You know what Czchlytski say," said Schwartz. "You read his book? Vhat is it vhat he say?"

"Oh, that's all right," answered Boggs, "if the game is worth the sacrifice. But here, you know — well, here it'd be like risking your neck to kill a dog."

"Vell, vhy make a risk? " said Schwartz.

"What do you mean?" asked Boggs, rather suspiciously.

"Send heem a pomb by mail," said Schwartz.

Boggs didn't seem to take kindly to the idea.

"It's easy," said Zimmerman, an enormously fat Low German. "Kraus done it in Bremen; didn't you, Kraus?"

Kraus nodded assent.

"Did you kill a man?" asked Boggs quickly.

"No," said Kraus, "de pomb didn't go off. But dat vasn't my fault. I loaded de tarn pipe, all right. I put gunpowder in it, *end* dynami-i-te. It didn't go off!"

Boggs ran his hands through his hair and then slowly reached for his glass and wetted his lips. The others watched him a narrowly and said nothing.

"I don't like to do it," he said at length. "It might—"

"Are you afrait?" asked Schwartz insinuatingly.

"Not a bit!" exclaimed Boggs, flushing. It was tauntingly asked, this question that, among companions such as he had, was an insult, and Boggs resented it enough to fling it back in Schwartz's teeth.

"You get the bomb," he said, straightening up, "and I'll look after sending it."

"Done," said Schwartz, banging the table with his fist. "I haf it here tomorrow."

"Tomorrow night?" said Boggs.

"Yes, sir."

"Here?"

"Yes, sir."

Boggs' eyes suddenly lighted again.

"What kind'll it be?" he asked.

"De regular kas-pipe kind," Schwartz. "Von inch acrost."

Boggs made a mental calculation.

"That's too big," he said. "I'll want a smaller one—say, half an inch or three-quarters thick—and two or three inches long."

Schwartz urged objections.

"It vouldn't do mooch tamage," he said.

"It'll do all I want," replied Boggs. "The way I'm going to fire it, it'd blow up a battleship."

"I make it fur you," said Schwartz. "I haf it here tomor-row."

Then Boggs went home and to bed, and, what may seem remarkable, to sleep.

NEXT MORNING, he took a long walk into the suburbs, to think. But, for some reason, his thoughts would not flow in an ordinary manner. A new development of his theory of national bank circulation occurred to him, and before long, he found that it was hopelessly entangled with an idea regarding the governmental control of bucket-shops. Then he tried to remember a paragraph he had read regarding the individual's right to existence, and it grew confused with thoughts of his coming trip to Europe. He decided that he would land at Cherbourg and make a tour on foot straight across the continent, and in a southeasterly direction, toward the Balkans. Soon he caught himself wondering if the ties on the railroads there were close enough together to make walking over them possible. If they were not, he decided, he would follow the highroads.

That afternoon, he worked in a sort of haze, like a drunken man, but no one seemed to notice it, for few members of the *Tribune* staff ever paid heed to him. Hemming may have noticed that his answers to the usual questions were more willing than usual, but, then, Hemming was not a very observant man, and his own affairs burdened his mind.

At half-past ten o'clock that night, Boggs closed his desk and left the office. He went to a rapid-fire lunchroom, and after upbraiding a waiter for making him wait three minutes for a soft-boiled egg, lingered over it an hour.

Then he proceeded to Bauermeister's saloon to meet Kraus and Schwartz and the rest.

Schwartz had the bomb in his pocket. At a casual glance, it appeared to be a bit of rusty iron gas pipe, sealed at both ends. It was about as long as a cigar, and slightly thicker. Boggs handled it gingerly.

"On dis ent," explained Schwartz, "iss de bercussion cap."

Boggs turned it over to see.

"You haf to trow it a goot distance," continued Schwartz, "or maybe it von't go off. Once Kraus made one like—"

"It'll get all the percussion it wants the way I'm going to throw it," said Boggs.

"Yes?" said Schwartz.

"You bet your whiskers," continued Boggs. "I'm going to give it a drop of sixty feet."

The others chuckled with professional admiration.

"I tropped one off a bridge onct," said Zimmerman. "Id fell two hundert foot—but it missed de train."

All laughed at this subtle joke, and Boggs wrapped the bomb in his handkerchief and put it into his pocket. The others affected to begin a conversation on other subjects, but it was plain that the proximity of the bomb did not add much to their comfort, and soon even Schwartz, who had made it and brought it in his pocket, grew restless. By and by, they went home, and Boggs left with them.

"Goot luck," said Zimmerman, as they parted at the street corner.

"Don't be skeert," cautioned Schwartz. "Rememper vhat Czchlytski says."

"So long," said Boggs. "I'll see you later."

THE NIGHT before, he had slept soundly, but now his eyes would not close, and he lay awake until dawn, trying to reconcile the jumbled ideas that arose within him. Once he half decided to throw the bomb into the river and face his martyrdom anew, but this plan was soon cast aside. Toward morning, he began to make a mental list of the clothes that he would need for his journey across the ocean, and to estimate their probable cost. This matter engaged him for several hours, and after the sun had risen, he fell asleep and slept until the chorus of factory whistles awakened him to tell him that it was noon.

Boggs bounded out of bed with a start, and angry that he had slumbered so long. Ordinarily, he reached the office at noon, and in all probability Hemming was already blowing loud blasts upon the speaking-tube whistle. It was a matter of a few minutes to dress and of another few minutes to hurry to the street corner. There, Boggs boarded a car and in a little while was downtown. Just as the sirens along the waterfront gave notice that it was half-past twelve, he entered his office and locked the door behind him. Then he took off his coat and vest, rolled up his sleeves, and vaulted to the top of a table that stood beside the tube. He drew forth the bomb from his hip pocket and raised the flexible end of the tube, so that it stretched upward from the tin section fastened to the wall.

The bomb would not go into the tube; the nickel whistle and mouthpiece blocked its way. Boggs tore off the mouthpiece and then put it loosely into its place again. Then he waited.

In a minute, there was a shrill whistle. It was the signal. Hemming was at the other end of the line—far below, on the first floor, four flights below the editorial rooms.

"Hello," said Boggs, as of old. "What is it?"

"How about Eye-ex-ell Irrigation 5's?" asked Hemming.

"Wait a minute and I'll see," answered Boggs.

And while Hemming waited, Boggs lifted the loosened mouthpiece from its place and slipped the iron cylinder into the orifice. It fitted quite snugly, though not tightly. After it had passed through the rubber section and entered the long tin cylinder that reached downstairs, it would move easily enough. All that was needed was to gently urge it at the start. Boggs decided that compressed air should be the motive power and his lungs the motor. The bomb was in the tube and the end was at his lips. He blew softly at first, and felt the iron cylinder slowly move through the rubber one. Then he took a long breath and blew hard, and the bomb jumped forward. In the tenth part of a second, it was at the bend in the tube, where the rubber section joined the tin. There was a sharp angle there, and the bomb struck it at good speed.

Something turned Boggs upside down just then, and he forgot Hemming and the bomb. It seemed as if a huge fly-wheel had seized him and were whirling him around at the rate of a thousand revolutions a second. A queer blue light flashed before him, and something hard struck his head. After a while, the blue light died out and it became dark and chilly.

Allen, the assistant city editor, and Oscar, the office boy, came running, for the something that struck Boggs made a loud noise. With a chair, they battered down his office door and sprang in upon him. He was as bloody as a butcher and apparently as dead as the day before yesterday.

In an ambulance, they took him to a hospital, and six weeks later, when he was able to walk again, he was given a pleasant room in the State Asylum for the Insane.

After all, Hemming was the chief loser, though not in the way Boggs thought he would be. By not receiving a prompt answer to his inquiry regarding Eye-ex-ell Irrigation 5's, he lost the sum of $74.50.

THE STAR-SPANGLED BANNER

"Stand back, let me hang my harp on the tree;
You are weary of the music it brings."
— J. Gordon Coogler

OF MUSIC, considered as a fine art, Messrs Brown and Tankersley knew less, it is probable, than any ordinary deck hand or ash man you might meet in a month's journey. Brown, by dint of much effort, could distinguish a waltz from a march, and Tankersley, having been an inmate at a time, for a season of three months, of a British military prison south of the Line, recognized "God Save the King" when he heard it, though, personally, he could not sing it, or even whistle it. Of skill in song and of the wisdom of fugues, cadenzas, and tempi, each was as innocent as the patriarchs. To their ears, the second act of *Tristan and Isolde* was noise, and the Pilgrim's Chorus mere sound. They were not musicians.

Nevertheless, when all is said, they knew enough about the divine art in its more practical aspects to direct the tour of an opera company, and this they had proved in the case of the Lyrico organization. Back at poor, lost St. Pierre, in Martinique, where the pop of the cork and the tinkle of the castanet ended in awful silence these many moons ago, they had assumed control and direction of it, thanks to a chain of circumstances, and throughout Jamaica and Cuba, which are islands of many virtues, it had appeared under their management with no small success. Of course, there had been exacting hotel-keepers and captious critics along the way, and they had encountered difficulties now and then, but to be in difficulties is the lot of the luckless impresario at all times and everywhere, and, one by one, their troubles had been met and conquered. Now, there was a fair balance to their credit in the branch Bank of Nova Scotia at Kingston, and they were beginning to acquire the polished affability and ease of manner that go with opulence.

The Señor Badajoz, the Castilian basso, was the cause of most of their early woes. Accordingly, they forcibly "released" him from his contract during the engagement of the company at the town of Montego Bay. Now, well rid of him, they were passengers on the tramp steamer *Cartagena,* bound westward across the upper end of the Spanish Main, toward Belize, in British Honduras. Three days were to be spent at Belize, and then there was to be a wait of four days for the steamer back across the emerald sea to Trinidad.

Messrs. Brown and Tankersley, seated upon the after-hatch of the *Cartagena* in pajamas and smoking greasy-looking Santa Clara cigars, were considering the plans for the Belize engagement.

"I vote in favor of *Carmen* as against *Tanhowser,*" said Brown. "It's got more swing to it, and what's more, it's Mexican, so to speak, with bullfighters and all that, and the greasers ought to like it. *Tanhowser's* nothin' but 'bing, bing!'"

"I guess you're right," said Tankersley reflectively. "And as for the other two nights?"

"*Trovytoar* and *The Bohemian Girl.*"

"Good," said Tankersley.

Brown had come to consider, with no small pride, his managerial acumen, and Tankersley, in a half-envious fashion, yielded to it, too. Hadn't Brown devised the scheme of giving the tower song in *Il Trovatore* in utter darkness, to hide the lack of scenery, and wasn't his the plan to have "The Tempest of the Heart" sung by a mixed chorus instead of by the baritone, when the voice of the Lyricio company's baritone grew so tuneless that the gallery in Mantanzas laughed at it?

"Touchin' on the basso business," resumed Brown, "it seems to me that we could get that guy, Declasse, to do the bellowin'. I talked to him the day after we bounced Badajoz, and he bucked at it. But I guess if it comes down to *must,* he can sing bass all right, just as good as he can sing tenor. He's fat enough."

Tankersley smiled with easy conviction.

"We can help him make up his mind," he said.

"And then," continued Brown, "we can let that little fellow, Labello, sing tenor. He's a tenor anyhow, he says, and the chorus can spare him. It's a waste of money carryin' a chorus around these way-stations."

"True enough," said Tankersley, in ready agreement, and then, for a space, the pair of impresarios smoked in silence and the little *Cartagena* wallowed along through the heavy Caribbean rollers, and from below decks came the smothered tones of a sea-sick soprano practicing scales. She was essaying a chromatic assent ascent in the key of F-sharp minor, from the middle of "C" to the upmost limit of her register, and Brown moved uneasily.

"It's that sort of squealing," he said gloomily, indicating with his thumb the region below him, "that knocks out the profit. What audiences want, as I figger it out, is *tune,* not *noise.* I've been thinkin' it over ever since we butted into the game, and it seems to me that some of those operas need a little overhaulin'."

"As to how?" asked Tankersley.

"They need to have a couple of good songs thrown in, here and there," replied Brown. "After the tenors and sopranos've been tearin' around for a while, the whole company ought to come down to the footlights and sing something catchy, like they do in civilized United States shows at home. There's a whole hour of 'bing, bing' in *Tanhowser,* f'r instance, without a single tune in it. You can't remember a note of it. The singers simply blaze away, and the fiddlers and so on scramble along after them. It's enough to drive a man to drink."

"Which it does," said Tankersley. "I've thought of the same thing myself, and I suppose other people have, too."

"There's our cue," said Brown, slapping his knee. "Other people have done the thinkin'. Now let us do the *doin'*."

Tankersley considered a moment.

"Could it be done?" he asked.

"Why not?" demanded Brown.

"Suppose the singers kick?" said Tankersley, tentatively. "What then? Suppose they refuse to sing anything but what's in the opera?"

Brown laughed the easy laugh of a man merciful to obstacles.

"Let them refuse!" he said. "Who pays their salaries? Who pays their freight? What would happen to 'em if we fired 'em? What happened to Badajoz? He went home in the steerage."

"But if we fired all of 'em," protested Tankersley, "we wouldn't have a company any more. We'd be out of work, so to speak."

"Leave that to me," said Brown grandly, and, forthwith, he slipped into his long raincoat, stalked forward, and entered into conversation with M. Declasse, who was leaning over the bow rail and gazing wearily and meditatively at the horizon. M. Declasse was at once interested in what he said, and soon the two were engaged in an absorbing argument. Brown endeavored to prove something and the tenor endeavored to combat it. They became much excited—particularly the tenor—and their voices rose above the swish and hum of the water under the bows and the dull beat of the engines.

"Eet vill cause ze insurrection!" protested M. Declasse.

"The what?" asked Brown.

"Ze revolution," replied the tenor. "Ze artists will decline to sing."

Brown puffed his cigar meditatively and smiled.

"They *will*, will they?" he drawled. "They will decline?"

"Oui, monsieur," replied M. Declasse.

"Then let them do it," said Brown grandly. "Let them *dare!*"

And this speech, which was in keeping with the majesty of an impresario, was the beginning for the Lyricio Opera Company of fresh troubles. M. Declasse repeated it to his fellow singers—Mme. Le Brun, the contralto; Mlle. Avignon, the "peerless soprano dramatique," and the others—and to the Señor Cardenas, the musical director, when they gathered on deck after dinner to admire the moon and sip their post-prandial cognac and coffee.

NEXT DAY also, after the *Cartagena* docked at Belize and the company was established at the leading hotel, Brown repeated it to them, and loud indeed were the murmurs of disapproval. But Brown heeded them not, for, as he carefully reminded them, Tankersley and he, in matters of management, were absolute monarchs, and, as such, were utterly indifferent to carping or other criticisms.

Nevertheless, before the rise of the curtain upon the first performance next evening, there was a sad scene upon the stage of Belize's house of public amusement, and, if the truth must be told, Brown and M. Declasse came to blows. Brown had selected two songs to be interpolated in *Carmen,* and Señor Cardenas, the musical director, who was in need of money and desired to retain his baton, had meekly arranged them. One was a gay and witty lyric in ragtime, and the other was a highly sentimental and chaste ditty regarding the charms of a certain Alice Jones, which had been the rage in Mobile the last time Brown had visited that pleasant little city.

M. Declasse refused point-blank to sing either of these

songs; first, on the ground that he was unable to pronounce English clearly and intelligibly, and, secondly, on the ground that if he essayed them in public, he would be disgraced for life. Thereupon, Brown grew excited and insistent, and the upshot of it all was an exchange of blows. The Señor Cardenas rushed up and separated the contestants in the nick of time, and Tankersley, who happened in, attempted to make peace.

"For the present," he said, "let us call it off. Tomorrow morning we can talk it over."

Then he whispered a few words to Brown, and the latter set off with him toward their hotel, while M. Declasse struggled into his costume with a feeling of high elation. He had won. The matter would be dropped. Also, there had been no further mention of his singing basso roles. The *Americano* swine had been silenced. There would be no desecration of the opera.

Herein, in truth, he was partly right, for *Carmen* was sung that night without American trimmings, and the vast audience favored M. Declasse with whirlwinds of applause. He had triumphed, and he was glad. It was a victory for the right. The American swine had been silenced.

In the meantime, while M. Declasse had been enjoying the applause of the audience and the audience had been enjoying his heavy warbling, Messrs. Brown and Tankersley had been closed in their room at the hotel with a compatriot named Ferguson. Ferguson was the manager and chief engineer of the Don Caesar and Little John copper mines, which lay, side by side, a twin wilderness of derricks and smokestacks and shanties, forty miles south of Belize, in the coast skirting the Cockscomb Mountains. As the crow flies, the distance from the Belize docks to Ferguson's office was forty miles. As the mere human being must travel, the distance was nearly a hundred miles—eighty-five miles down the zig-zag coast to the wharf called Port

Smith, and fifteen miles up from the sea by the narrow-gauge railway which brought the ore to the cargo ships. Ferguson was explaining the geography of it.

"You see," he said, "it takes a day to get here from the mines, and a day to get back. That makes two days. All of the chaps up at the mines would like to hear your company sing, but it wouldn't do, of course, for all of them to come down here on a two-days' trip. Before they got back, they might put the town on the bum, and the greasers might play the deuce with the machinery. And if I let half of them come down to Belize, and make the other half stay up at the mines, there'd be trouble in carloads. It wouldn't work at all."

"I see," said Brown.

"I'm on," said Tankersley.

"And so it struck me," said Ferguson, "that, if the consideration was big enough, you might find it possible to bring the company up to the mines. You've got a week to wait for the steamer and the trip's an easy one. Altogether, there are sixty of us up there—sixty white men—fifty Americans and a few Englishmen and Canadians—and we're willing to put up a ten-spot apiece. That's six hundred, gold. Could you do it?"

"The money," said Brown, "to be paid in advance?"

"Around the corner at the bank," said Ferguson. "Now."

And so the bargain was made, and Ferguson and the managers of the Lyrico Opera Company conferred regarding the matter of the details. After the third performance at Belize, it was decided, the company was to embark in the mine company's steamer, *Sweet Alice,* which was to land the singers at Port Smith at noon. Then they were to journey to the mines in a special train of carpeted and awninged ore cars, and that afternoon, in an old, converted sugar mill on the mines' property, they were to give a performance. After the final curtain, they were to be reconveyed to the coast by the special train, and put aboard the *Sweet Alice,* which was to land them at Belize again next morning. It was a simple arrangement and eminently satisfactory.

Regarding the matter of the entertainment they were to furnish, Ferguson had positive orders. There must be one or two good, loud quartets; a couple of classical numbers to give tone to the affair; three or four arias from the comic operas; and last, but far from least, a half-dozen patriotic songs.

"Some of those chaps up there," explained Ferguson, "haven't heard 'The Star Spangled Banner' for five years. They're almost as homesick for it as they are for a good American beefsteak."

Messrs. Brown and Tankersley agreed to the arrangements without argument, and after Ferguson, with the simplicity of the expatriated American, had handed them a New York draft for $600 gold, they set out, with the honesty of the expatriated American—and, after cashing the draft at the Colonial Bank—to carry out the terms of their contract.

As they half expected, M. Declasse interposed serious objections. In the first place, he pointed out, he had not been engaged for a concert tour. He was an opera singer—an artist—and did not propose to debase himself by singing ballads like a low, cheap barnstormer or vaudeville.

In the second place, his contract did not call for his appearance in cities not marked upon the map. Was there an opera house at the Don Caesar and Little John mines? If there was, he never had heard of it.

In the third place, he did not propose to risk his life and limb upon the journey. He had seen the steamer, *Sweet Alice,* at the Belize dock. It was a condemned and greasy ocean tug filled with engines and unpleasant odors.

In the fourth place, the proposition that he sing American national airs was absurd. He could not speak English well enough to remember the words, and he had no desire to do so. He was a Frenchman, not an Englishman or an

American, and the only languages he cared to know with any degree of perfection were French, Italian, and Spanish.

Messrs. Brown and Tankersley informed M. Declasse that he was a clown and a knave, and that his ingratitude pained them.

"Haven't we fed you and kept you alive?" demanded Brown. "Didn't we pick you up when you were on your uppers back there in St. Pierre, and haven't we paid you your salary every week since? Haven't we treated you like a white man? Didn't we let you have your own way the other night when you refused to sing the songs I picked out for *Carmen?*"

"Zere, I vanqueeshed you," said M. Declasse grandly.

"Did you?" exclaimed Brown. "Well, we'll see if you did. We'll show you!"

And then Messrs. Brown and Tankersley left him and he went among the company and spread the insurrection that he had promised.

That afternoon—it was the day of the Lyricio Company's last performance at Belize—the singers held a meeting at the hotel and formally agreed to refuse absolutely to go to Port Smith. A few moments before the rise of the curtain that evening, M. Declasse sought out Brown and informed him of their decision.

"In that case," answered Brown genially, "I am sorry to inform you that there will be trouble. Meanwhile, I suppose, you will not object to my consulting Mr. Tankersley before giving you our answer."

"I haf not ze objection," replied M. Declasse.

So Brown conferred with Tankersley, and the result of their conference was the dispatch of a telegram to Ferguson, at the mines. Thus it read:

"Can't bring women. Will men do alone?"

An hour later, just as the curtain fell upon the first act of the opera, there came Ferguson's answer:

"Want all, if possible. If not, bring men, dead or alive."

Then, Messrs. Brown and Tankersley went to M. Declasse's dressing room and presented him with their ultimatum.

"We've decided," said Brown, "that the date at the mines must be filled. The steamer will leave at midnight and we'll expect you boys to be aboard by eleven-forty-five. That's all."

M. Declasse laughed derisively as he changed his costume, and all during the next act he smiled as he sang. During the third act, also, he smiled, and the other singers, whom he had informed of the manager's speech, smiled too. Fifteen minutes after the fall of the last curtain, however, M. Declasse ceased to smile, and the others ceased with him. Just as he, M. Declasse, had removed the last vestige of greasepaint from the fringes of his Van Dyke beard, and was struggling into his tuxedo, Brown appeared in the doorway of his dressing room and pointed a pistol at his head.

"Come along," said Brown simply.

"Eh?" gasped M. Declasse in surprise.

"Come along!" said Brown.

And M. Declasse came along.

On the cleared stage, the women of the company stood about in dumb terror, and the men stared, speechless. In close proximity to each of the latter—there were eleven altogether—stood a ruffian with a pistol. Tankersley was nearest to the Señor Cardenas. The other ruffians—who seemed to be the *Americanos* who loafed at the hotel and drank brandy and soda with Brown and Tankersley—looked after the other singers.

"March!" said Brown, and the entire party, captives and captors, marched out of the stage door and down the narrow street to the wharf behind the opera house. At the wharf, in the witching, tropical moonlight, lay the steamer *Sweet Alice,* belching smoke.

The party marched aboard without a sound and the women of the company, who had followed after, stood on the wharf in petrified silence. Then all of the ruffians but two went ashore, the steamer's propeller kicked round, she moved away from the wharf, and Brown and Tankersley and the two remaining ruffians laughed.

All that night, M. Declasse, the Señor Cardenas and the other singers and musicians lay on deck in the chilly land breeze and the *Americanos* played cards in the chart room.

At dawn, the first long splinter of light from the east showed the Coxscomb Mountains on the starboard bow, and at eight o'clock, after the half-breed cook had served a breakfast of tinned peaches and crackers, the *Sweet Alice* edged in toward the dock at Port Smith, and M. Declasse, the Senor Cardenas, *et al.*, marched ashore.

Then they climbed aboard three awninged flatcars and clutched the rope railings, and for three hours thereafter they held on in fear while the little train swung round wobbly, narrow-gauge curves and crawled over tall, shaky trestles, and painfully puffed its way up the mountainside, through thickets of bananas and bamboos and strange plants that arched over the track and made the right of way a tunnel. Once, the engine halted near the crest of a hill and the passengers were required to detrain and walk. As they stumbled along the weed-grown pathway between the rails, Brown reminded M. Declasse that his singing of "The Star Spangled Banner" was expected to be the "hit" of the entertainment.

"Ze song, I do not know," replied M. Declasse doggedly.

"You lie," replied Brown, "I've heard you hum it."

"Ah, zat ees ze moosic," said M. Declasse. "Ze wairds, I know not."

"Who said you did?" exclaimed Brown. "Nobody wants

you to sing the words. Nobody can understand the words of a song you sing, anyhow. Blaze away with any old words. Tra-la-la — and so on. *Sabe?"*

"Diablo!" said M. Declasse, climbing aboard the train again.

In another hour, the party arrived at the railhead, which was also the center of the *Americanos'* city of derricks and shafts, and the *Americanos* themselves, lined up on both sides of the track in red shirts, khaki, dress-coats, silk hats, and other varied holiday garb, gave them a rousing cheer. Brown and Tankersley smilingly raised their hats in ac-knowledgment and shook hands with Ferguson, and then the *Americanos* aided the singers, who were glum and smileless, to alight. A gaily-decorated six-mule ore wagon, with improvised seats, was beside the track, and into it the singers and their *Americano* managers were lifted bodily, and with the sixty *Americanos* of the mines and their two hundred Indo-Spanish-American assistants marching ahead and behind as a guard of honor, the party was con-veyed to the "opera house." The audience was impatient. There was no time to waste. The show should begin at once.

A corps of peons had swept and furnished the old sugar mill — said relic of the good old days when sugar was king — and from its crumbling walls hung festoons of palm branches and banana "fans" and clusters of tiger-lilies and other gaudy flowers of the tropics. At one end, the mechan-ical staff of the mine had erected a stage with wings, oil-lamp footlights, though it was broad daylight, and a cur-tain like a real theater at home.

Through a side door, Messrs. Brown and Tankersley and their singers were led to the region behind the curtain, and the sixty *Americanos* and their two hundred Indo-Spanish-American assistants crowded into the auditorium. Outside, the engines in the power houses at the mine entrances were still, and the mules grazed peacefully in the corral. The

Don Caesar and Little John copper mines, for the first time since the day they were opened, were having a holiday. In three hours, they would come to life again. Their servants and attendants, while they lay motionless, were determined to be merry.

Amid a storm of loud applause and festive yells, the four-man orchestra struggled round to the space before the curtain and plunged into the intricacies of the overture *William Tell*. This composition is scored for many more instruments than two violins, one cornet, and a clarinet, but, despite the demerits of its interpretation, the applause that greeted it was fairly thunderous, and the orchestra was compelled, almost by brute force, to respond with another selection.

Then, the Señor Miguel Janenos, baritone dramatique, stepped before the footlights and warbled an aria from *Faust*. Five times, he was called back to warble anew, until, by and by, he staggered off the stage, exhausted.

Then came the next victims, MM. Leon and de Lasselles, in a duet, and soon the audience became so enthusiastic that the end of each number was the beginning of a wild outburst of cheers and yells and stamping of feet and clapping of hands.

Some of the auditors had not heard civilized music for three years, and others—old engineers and mine bosses—not for five years. Now, were it not for the gray walls of the mill and the palms without, they might imagine themselves back again in Boston or Chicago or London or Toronto, or wherever it was that there existed the bricks and mortar that made their home. It was royal, it was great, it was bully!—and they were enjoying it to the full.

Meanwhile, behind the scenes, Messrs. Brown and Tankersley were having trouble. M. Declasse once more was in rebellion. It was on account of the matter of "The Star Spangled Banner." In a few moments he was to "go on" and sing it, and now he was in the act of declaring that he would never do so.

Brown and Tankersley withdrew to a corner of the region behind the curtain and conferred. Five minutes later, M. de Laselles, having completed the singing of the toreador's song from *Carmen,* bounded from the stage, and it was M. Declasse's turn to appear.

"March!" said Brown, approaching him.

"I know not ze wairds," protested M. Declasse obstinately.

Brown and Tankersley simultaneously drew deadly weapons from their hip pockets—the same short, brutal, melodramatic revolvers they had handled back in Belize.

"March!" said Brown.

M. Declasse gazed at the weapons nervously, but held to his declaration.

"I know not ze wairds," he protested.

"Then sing any old words," said Brown. "I've told you that. Now, march!"

M. Declasse looked at the revolvers again—their muzzles were rising to the level of his head—and then he bethought him of a plan to save his honor—the honor of a Frenchman and a gentleman. Yes, he would sing the vile song, but he would sing it in his own way. He would show his contempt for the *Americanos* and their dirty rag of a flag while they—poor clowns—were congratulating themselves upon making what they thought was a conquest of him.

M. Declasse's indignation gave way to grim joy, and the grim joy grew so great that it buried his reason and his common sense, and, so, when he marched out to the center of the stage, with a revolver gleaming in each wing, and the audience arose en masse and shouted itself hoarse and breathless, he smiled and bowed and grimaced, for he looked upon himself as the victor. The *Americanos* in the audience, like the *Americanos* behind the revolvers in the wings, were dogs and swine, and in a contest with a French gentleman, were like little children. He would make fools of them while they thought he was complimenting them, and the story would be a good one to tell over the absinthe when he got back to Paris and civilization and the society of human beings.

Thus M. Declasse walked to the center of the stage, bowing and smiling, and thus he burst into the music of "The Star Spangled Banner." Loudly, the orchestra banged out the accompaniment, and, loudly, the audience cheered.

"Oh, zay, can you zee—"

So began M. Declasse, for he knew the first line, and then, with a soft chuckle, he set out to sing the balance of it according to his own plan. Brown had said that "any old words" would do, in "any old language." "Sing trala-la," were the words of Brown. M. Declasse would improve on them. He would sing in Spanish, and he would improvise words and sentiments as he proceeded. Madrid had not applauded him as an *improvisatore* in vain. So on he sang, and this is a free translation of what he sang, in good Castilian, with the least bit of a French accent:

> The *Americanos* are swine and caitiffs and dogs;
> They have the manners of degraded beasts.
> They are cowards and enemies of righteousness;
> Their faces are the faces of dumb brutes;
> In valor, a hundred *Americanos* are the equal of one
>   Frenchman.
> They are murderers, thieves, rascals and—

THREE DAYS later, M. Declasse landed at Belize with his right arm in a rude sling and many yards of gauze bandage wrapped about his head. It had taken him a day to journey from Port Smith to Belize on an ore steamer. The other two days he had spent in the jungle, slowly making his way on foot toward the coast. He had slept on the ground and had gone foodless, and so it happened that he was sadly used up and sadly out of humor.

Messrs. Brown and Tankersley, who met him at the Belize wharf, were equally damaged. Brown, when the crash came and the audience rose to mutilate and slay, had dashed out of the opera house by way of a side door, and, that night, had met Tankersley on the wagon road to the coast, five miles from the mines. The Señor Cardenas and his musicians had been pursued across country for ten miles by a party of *Americanos* on mule-back and had twice given up hope of ever reaching civilization again. But now all, including M. de Laselles, M. Leon, and the others, were safe, though perhaps not entirely sound, in Belize again, and Messrs. Brown and Tankersley were tearing their hair.

M. Declasse, through loudly asserted that it was not his fault.

"Ze zwine beat me!" he exclaimed. "Zey knock me ovaire! Zey strike me wis logs uf vood! Zey—"

And M. Declasse fairly wept.

"It was your fault, you villain!" exclaimed Brown. "You insulted 'em! You insulted *me!* Didn't you have sense enough to know that they could understand Spanish?"

"You zay to me, 'Zing anysing,'" protested M. Declasse.

The ladies of the company, who had been left behind, came running from the hotel to comfort Monsieur.

"Poor darling!" exclaimed Mme. Le Brun.

"The wretches!" exclaimed Mlle. Avignon.

They petted the luckless M. Declasse and wept upon his shoulder, and Messrs. Brown and Tankersley looked on in disgust.

"I feel like punching his head," said Brown.

Tankersley lighted a cigar and flickered the match into the water.

"What's the use?" he said. "We've got the six hundred."

"And lucky we are to have it," said Brown.

THE KING & TOMMY CRIPPS

Calm-eyed, he scoffs at sword and crown,
Or, panic-minded, stabs and slays:
Blatant, he bids the world bow down,
Or, cringing, begs a crumb of praise—
An American

TOMMY CRIPPS was one of those uncompromising Americans who indignantly spurn all temptations to belong to other nations. He had two large, white teeth in the very center of his upper jaw, and his ears, viewed from behind, seemed to meet his head at something approaching a right angle. All of this gave him an air of quite startling ferocity, to which his assertive, resourceful, cocksure manner lent color.

He believed that the United States, in some mysterious fashion, governed and regulated the rest of the world, and in proof of its supremacy, he was wont to cite the fact that he, himself, had never met defeat in physical combat at the hands of any foreign boy of his age, whether Frenchman, German, Italian, Russian, or Spaniard.

Tommy was twelve and he had good, strong legs and muscles in his arms that he delighted to show. His greatest exploit, all things considered, was his defeat of two little Austrian dukes at San Remo. He had met them on the esplanade in front of the Grand Hotel, estrayed from their tutor, and on their commenting adversely upon the cut of his Norfolk jacket, he had seized them by their royal necks and struck their aristocratic heads together.

Despite the frequent chances it gave him to help impress upon the world a realization of the fearful might of Uncle Sam, Tommy did not like the idea of traveling about Europe. His mother, too, felt that it had its disadvantages, for hotel life was making a spoiled, domineering, boastful boy of him, and it was frequently necessary for his father to chastise him, which is an operation painful to all concerned. But this traveling had to be done nevertheless, for Mr. Cripps was some sort of agent for a large steel works at home, and it was part of his work to journey hither and thither over half the continent, conferring with ministers of public improvements and railroad directors and stout apoplectic merchant princes.

Tommy and Tommy's mother went with him, up and down over the land, from the Baltic to the Dardanelles. Tommy used to spell out the long words in the *Paris Herald* and *London Times* and wish he could go back to the land where every person one met spoke real English, and every boy knew the difference between a baseball and a bat.

This traveling had continued for three years, and Tommy remembered three days that had seemed peculiarly desolate and gloomy. Each of these had been a Fourth of July. The first had been spent by the Cripps family at Christiania, in Norway, where it was cold and cheerless, and the second at Rome, where there was much speech-making by a lot of old fogies and discordant patriotic song-singing, not to mention the sentimental drinking of rye whisky. The third Fourth was passed, miserably, in a train on the great Siberian railway, somewhere between Moscow and Omsk, where Mr. Cripps was going to look into the building of a steel bridge. The utter gloom and anguish of that day, with its dull panorama of rolling steppe, made Tommy resolve that if he lived to see another Fourth, he would make it glorious. He was tired of quiet and weariness on his country's birthday. He wanted firecrackers and red fire and parades and all that sort of thing.

Being an American of action, and having cunning of the kind that a small boy develops when he is left too much to his own devices, he began preparations a good while in advance. At Paris, where his father was detained most of the winter, he laid in a small stock of little American flags, and in London, where he spent a week, he bought a miniature toy cannon.

In London, too, he made the purchase which delighted him most of all. It consisted of a package of half a dozen big firecrackers—big red ones of the kind that blow off the fingers of boys at home. Tommy found them at a store devoted to the sale of Chinese goods, and the man refused to sell them, as he said, to "a child." This sent Tommy back to the hotel for an old friend, the under-porter, who in consideration of sixpence in hand, went to the store, represented him in the transaction, and turned the crackers over to him.

Tommy hid them with the cannon and the flags and his tin soldiers in the bottom of the satchel that held his school books. This was in March, and thereafter, for three months or more, he successfully distracted from them the attention of the customs officials of five nations. Once, on the Belgian frontier, a rude functionary in red whiskers plunged his hand into the satchel and felt about. Tommy's heart was in his mouth, for he thought that the firecrackers, because they were American, would have to pay enormous duties, and he was afraid that his father might take them away from him and treat him to the bastinado for carrying them. But, after a moment, the red-whiskered officer passed on, and, thereafter, there was no trouble, and the Fourth of July approached, and Tommy got ready.

Mr. Cripps, one day, told him that they would spend the glorious holiday in the capital of one of the seven-and-thirty lesser German kingdoms. Tommy remembered it as a dull and commonplace old town with crooked streets and high, overhanging houses, and he knew that there would be no other American boys at the hotel to help him celebrate. But he had got half used loneliness, and had begun to cease thinking of it. If need be, he would celebrate the day single-handed and alone, either on the street, on the roof, or in his room, and the celebration would be the best that old Rheinstadt ever knew.

THE CRIPPSES arrived early on the morning of the Fourth and engaged rooms at the gloomy old Rheinstadter Hof, the only hotel in the place. For Rheinstadt, the streets seemed lively, despite a fine rain that made little pools between the ancient cobblestones and damped the uniform of glorious *Polizei.*

There were crowds of wooden-shod, heavy-faced townspeople everywhere, and the *Polizei*, afoot and on horseback, kept dashing up and down, waving their short swords and looking as important and ferocious as could be. The man who kept the hotel told Mr. Cripps that King Ferdinand XVIII, of Lippe-Hochheim (which was the kingdom that had Rheinstadt for its capital) was coming home that afternoon and that his loyal subjects were assembled to greet him. A large portrait of his majesty hung in the parlor of the Rheinstadter Hof. It showed him to be a tall gentleman with a long, gray beard, wearing a feather in the side of his Alpine hat. Tommy had seen kings before, and this one lost nothing by comparison with the others. Most of the latter were lean and consumptive-looking or fat and squat. Few inspired much admiration in the breast of a patriotic American.

Tommy wanted to fare forth into the crowd and see the show, but Mr. Cripps, as a punishment for a minor misdemeanor of the day before, condemned him to go to the dull old *Thiergarten,* to look at the strange beasts from the Congo and Mesopotamia. Tommy cried and stamped his foot, but his father dragged him off, and they spent the forenoon tramping the wet gravel walks between the cages, Mr.

Cripps explaining the nature of each particular beast and Tommy thinking of the Fourth of July celebration that was dying abornin'. But, at midday, when they returned to the hotel, there appeared the American consul, who was by nationality a Swede, with an invitation for Mr. and Mrs. Cripps to eat a German dinner with him at his lodgings at two o'clock. It was accepted, and Tommy was left in his room at the Rheinstadter Hof, a book called *Harvey's Grammar* to read, and a caution to remain indoors until his father and mother returned.

"Can't I go out and look at the parade?" he asked pleadingly.

"You can look at the parade from the window," said Mr. Cripps.

Tommy sulked a while and then, in despair, he searched in his satchel for his precious treasures. There they were, below the schoolbooks and the tin soldiers, six round, red crackers, a little bundle of flags, and the toy cannon. Tommy took them out and ranged them on the table. One of the crackers, he discovered, was mashed, and the powder was leaking from it. With his jack-knife, he ripped the casing and gathered all of the powder upon a piece of paper. Then he loaded his toy cannon with it and rammed it home. The scratch of a match, a splutter, and — *bang!*

It wasn't as loud as the big guns of the *Oregon,* but it was a good, hearty *bang!*

Tommy listened for a moment to see if the report would attract any of the hotel porters, but, apparently, the shouts and clatter of hoofs in the plaza outside had drowned it. So he opened the window to let the stifling smoke out and prepared to have his little celebration there and then, regardless of the flogging it might bring when his father returned.

Cracker number two — the second of the six — sacrificed its young life in a dismal fizzle, and Tommy resolved to dissect the third, as he had done the first, and to load its powder in his cannon. Just as he began to work upon it, there was a great tumult in the plaza, and he ran to the window to see what had happened.

Below him—four stories below—was the crowd that had begun gathering all day, and through the middle of it ran a lane lined by *Polizei* on horseback. The king had arrived, and there, coming down the crooked old street that led from the railroad station, was his carriage. Ten horsemen, in bedraggled plumes and spangles, rode in front of it, and fifty behind, and on each side there were close ranks of *Polizei* and soldiers. It was a royal progress, and despite the fine rain and the glistening pools between the cobblestones, it made a show of magnificence. Tommy leaned far out of the window to watch it.

The carriage proceeded slowly until it came to the plaza, and then it started to cross, with its horses at a light trot, toward the street which led to the palace. Tommy craned his neck to see the king, but the carriage windows were closed and the guards' swords touched the very wheels. Suddenly, as he looked, the idea seized him, an idea that made his untamed American blood leap with joy. He would awaken Rheinstadt like a thunderclap! He would make the sleepy old city sit up and stare!

Out, then, from his pocket came a match, and *scratch* it went upon the window sill. Then the flame touched the fuse of the third cracker, the fuse sputtered—and Tommy threw the cracker far out into space. For a second or so, he watched it as it fell, turning over and over and sending forth a thin tail of little red sparks. The *Polizei* saw it, too, and one of them jumped in the air to grab it as it neared the ground. But he was too late, and, with a thunderous report, it exploded directly beside the driver of the king's carriage and almost under the off horse's hoofs. Then the crowd yelled, the *Polizei* drew their short swords, the king's horses reared and pranced, and his majesty, long of beard and white of face, bounded out into the street.

"Anarchists!" shouted the crowd.

"Back!" shouted the *Polizei.*

The king looked about him as if he were half dazed, and a dozen soldiers closed in about him. And, simultaneously, there was a general tumult. Horses reared, soldiers flashed their swords, officers shouted orders back and forth, and the crowd yelled and struggled and fought and roared.

"Death to the anarchists!" howled a man beside him, and the cry was taken up by the crowd.

But where were the anarchists? No one could find them. Whence had come the bomb? No one knew. Suddenly, the corporal of *Polizei* who had grabbed it remembered that it had come down from above. He looked up—and saw Tommy Cripps in the act of launching another one.

Two minutes later, three soldiers, excited and out of breath, smashed the door of Tommy's room and rushed at him with fixed bayonets.

"What do you want?" demanded Tommy in belated terror.

The soldiers sprang upon him, and his arms were pinioned behind him. Out in the hallway, with three other soldiers, was the proprietor of the hotel, pinioned also. He was crying loudly and protesting that Tommy had ruined him. Tommy himself, for the moment, was too scared to cry.

But, in a moment, his native pugnacity and degenerate brashness came to his rescue. He struggled with his captors and tried to break his bonds.

"Lemme go!" he screamed. "Lemme go, I tell you! My father'll break your heads! Lemme go!"

The soldiers apparently did not hear him. On the table beside him was the remainder of his stock of ordnance—the toy cannon and his three big red crackers. One of the soldiers gathered up the crackers gingerly and the others pushed Tommy out of the room ahead of them.

Down the long stairs they went, to the street. At the entrance to the hotel, there was a great, surging crowd, shouting lustily, and when Tommy appeared, manacled and white-faced, the people made a rush for him, crying, "Down with the anarchists!" Those who were near enough to actually see him marveled at his youth and made guesses as to his nationality, but the majority could only see the waving plumes upon the helmets of the soldiers in charge of him.

The *Polizei*—there were scores of them by now—held the struggling Rheinstadters back and Tommy was bundled into a dark, barred wagon. Then the horses were lashed, the wagon lurched forward, and there began a wild, rough ride over medieval cobblestones. Tommy was growing thoroughly frightened and, in a moment, he feared, he might begin to cry. The celebration had long since passed the patriotic stage.

After a while, the wagon halted in what seemed to be the courtyard of a huge jail, and Tommy was dragged forth and led into a large, gloomy room with bars at the windows. At a desk sat a tall man with a bristling military mustache and a gaudy green uniform, and beside him was another and even taller man, with a beard like the king's and a red uniform heavy with gold cords and ribbons and medals. Half a dozen soldiers, with rifles at the carry, stood at either side of them.

"It is for your excellency to interrogate the prisoner," said the first man, in German, and with a deferential air.

His excellency glared at Tommy.

"What is your name?" he demanded, also in German.

Tommy shook his head. He understood German, but the tall man scared him.

His excellency repeated the question in English.

"Thomas George Cripps," replied the boy.

"He's a mere child," observed the green uniformed man.

"I am twelve," said Tommy.

"Your nationality?" demanded his excellency.

"United States," answered Tommy, and the man in green wrote it down.

The tall man with the medals stroked his beard for a moment and contemplated his prisoner meditatively.

"Are you an anarchist?" he asked.

"A what?" replied Tommy.

"An anarchist."

"What's that?"

His excellency deigned to smile.

"A man," he said, "that throws bombs at kings."

"I didn't throw any bombs," protested Tommy, gradually regaining his assurance.

His excellency laughed again. He had a most evil laugh.

"You better let me go!" exclaimed Tommy explosively. "I ain't done anything!"

"We shall see," answered his excellency, majestically.

"Why don't you let me go?" cried Tommy.

"Because you are accused of trying to kill the king," replied his excellency.

Tommy's heart sank to his shoes. He remembered stories, clandestinely read, in which innocent persons were accused of all sorts of crimes and tortured with ghastly cruelty. They were attempting to distort the harmless explosion of a firecracker—"just fun," as Tommy put it—into murder.

"Lemme go!" he cried. "Lemme go! My father'll have you arrested—"

His tears overcame him as the desk telephone before his excellency jingled, and the rest of his speech was lost. There were three short, sharp jingles, and his excellency sprang to the instrument and glued his ear to the receiver. The three jingles were a warning that the king was at the other end of the line, and it behooved all who heard them to hasten and harken.

"Yes, your majesty," said his excellency, talking into the phone.

"The prisoner seems to be a mere child . . . no, not an evil face . . . rather impudent . . . an American, of course . . . I beg pardon? . . . Half a dozen, I fancy . . . scared, but brazen . . . denies any connection with Rugio and Lispiani . . . may I ask? . . . No, your majesty . . . to the palace? . . . at once, sir . . . at once . . . ."

His excellency turned from the telephone and gave an order in German.

"You are to be taken before his majesty, the king," he said to Tommy.

Tommy's face brightened. Kings, he remembered, always played the role of fairy deliverer. He would confound his enemies. He would be triumphantly acquitted—

But, just as he was being led from the room, his heart sank again, for a soldier grabbed him from behind and he was held firmly. Someone had remembered that the prisoner had not been searched, and here he was about to go into the presence of the king with a gun, perhaps, or maybe a dozen of them, concealed in his clothes! His excellency muttered something about a *dummer Narr*, and the other officer colored.

A short, squat soldier carefully felt in all of Tommy's pockets and dragged forth their contents. An American boy's pockets—and those of any other boy, for that matter—are his safe-deposit vaults, and Tommy's were laden with the spoil of Europe. There was a bit of colored stone from Pompeii, a curious brass key filched from a hotel at Venice, three English pennies with holes in them, the main fly-wheel of an American dollar watch, a bundle of colored cord, half a dozen odd buttons, two bent nails, an artist's thumbtack, a lead wheel from a toy locomotive, three tin soldiers, all rough-riders, the stump of a lead pencil, and a dried and petrified sponge.

Tommy protested loudly against being robbed of these treasures, and as he saw the fly-wheel of the dollar watch drop into the big red envelope in the officer's hands, he once more came near shedding tears.

But, soon, his native self-possession grew strong again and he decided that, come what may, it would not do to show the white feather in the presence of foreigners—particularly on the Fourth of July. And so he marched bravely on, like a patriot to the gibbet, and entered again the black wagon with the barred window.

THE DISTANCE to the palace, apparently, was not great, for the wagon stopped in a few moments, and Tommy was taken out and led into a huge room with vast paintings on the walls. One of the paintings represented the beheading of a pale young man with long hair and a ruffled shirt, and it made Tommy shudder.

In a moment, the same tall, gray-bearded man who had been in the carriage on the plaza came into the room, and the officers who guarded Tommy bowed low. He was the king, and he motioned them to go. When they had disappeared down the corridor, he asked Tommy to sit down, and pulled up another chair near him.

"So, you are the anarchist?" he said with a smile.

Tommy had seen a good many kings, and shoals of lesser royalties, but this was the first time that one of them had addressed a word to him directly, and despite his assertive democracy, he was somewhat awed.

"I ain't an anarchist," he replied in a faint, scared voice. "I'm just a boy. Those men robbed me."

"What men?" asked the king.

"Those men that brought me here to see you," replied

Tommy. "They took my wheel and my stone from Pompeii. They grabbed me and squeezed my arm."

The king arose and laughed.

"But you threw a bomb at me," he said. Tommy noticed that he spoke English with the soft accent of an Englishman.

"It wasn't a bomb," he protested. "It was a shooting-cracker. It was one of those big double-Dutchmen."

"Why did you throw it at me?" asked the king solemnly. "Didn't you know it might hurt me? Had I injured you in any way?"

For the first time, Tommy began to see that there might be an unmanly side to his Adventure, and he was ashamed. He hung his head and was silent.

"How would you like it," continued the king in his soft, gentle voice, "If I were to throw a bomb under the hoofs of your horses and scare you?"

Tommy, by now, was frankly embarrassed, and felt his cheeks burn red.

"Did it—scare you?" he asked.

The king stroked his long beard and the ghost of a smile played in his eyes.

"Yes," he answered judicially. "I was scared. I feared that anarchists were after my life. When a man is king, you know, he has to think of such things. It's not a pleasant trade."

Tommy saw a way to divert the discussion from his own misdemeanor.

"Don't you like being a king?" he asked blandly.

"Really, I haven't given the matter much thought," replied his majesty. "Even if I didn't like it, it would be hard, you know, to give the office to someone else. In your country, a man is not made a president unless he asks for the place, or at least, not unless he is known to want it. But on this side of the ocean, rulers are chosen in a different way.

If you were my son, now, you would be king when I died."

"Have you got a son?" asked the cunning Tommy.

And now it was the king's turn to change the subject. His son? His boy? No other father, he sometimes thought, ever had such a useless, profligate, dissolute son as the crown prince of Lippe-Hochheim. The gatekeepers of the Riviera met him oftener than his father. The ballet girls of London and Berlin knew him better; the *boulevardiers* of Paris were more his friends. The king's face clouded and he did not answer Tommy's question.

"But why," he asked instead, "why did you drop that bomb, or shooting-cracker, or whatever it was, from the hotel window?"

"Because it was the Fourth of July,"' replied Tommy simply. "Everybody at home shoots off shooting-crackers on the Fourth of July."

"Why?" asked the king.

Tommy glanced up at him in surprise.

The idea of a man, even a foreigner, who didn't know the significance of the Fourth of July was too much for him.

"Did you never hear of George Washington?" he asked.

"Yes," said the king. "I have heard of him."

"Well, the Fourth of July is the day he drove the English out of the country."

The king suppressed a smile.

"Washington was a great man," he observed.

"Yes," said Tommy, "he was the man that defeated the English. He beat them and kicked them out and they went back to England. At home, the people are so glad of it that they raise a big rumpus every year. They have fireworks and speeches and the bands play and it's a holiday. Everybody has a holiday on the Fourth of July."

"I see," said the king. "And you wanted to have a holiday, too?"

"That's it," said Tommy, glad that his august pupil had

grasped the idea. "I was all by myself and I wanted to have a little fun."

"And so you dropped your shooting-cracker in front of my carriage?"

Tommy's eyes fell, and he was uncomfortable once more. This king was a nice old man; he was sorry that he had scared him.

"And they arrested you?" continued his majesty.

"Yes, sir," said Tommy. "They grabbed me and stole everything I had in my pockets."

"Too bad!" said the king. "Too bad! I'll have them give it all back to you."

"You will?" exclaimed Tommy delightedly. "Thank you, sir. I'm much obliged."

"If you'll promise," continued the king, "that you won't drop shooting-crackers on me any more."

"I didn't mean to hurt you," said Tommy, sincerely repentant. "I just wanted to shoot off my shooting-crackers. When you came along, and I saw that crowd—well, I dropped one of them out of the window. I only did it in fun."

"But you must be careful not to bother kings," said his majesty. "It's a bad business, my boy. If you had hurt me, I might have had to clap you into jail. Suppose you had killed me?"

Tommy shuddered.

"What then?"

Tommy did not know.

"They would have put you into jail for the rest of your life."

Tommy considered a moment.

"I think you're wrong there," he said with naive impudence. "You might clap me in jail, but I'd get out again."

The king seemed vastly amused, and Tommy hastened to impress him with the gravity of the situation.

"Did you ever see the battleship *Oregon?*" he asked.

The king said that he had not.

"Well, then," said Tommy, "you ought to see her. We rowed to look at her at Naples. Her guns are as long—well, as from here to there," and he pointed to the far end of the room. "They shoot fifteen miles."

The king's eyes asked a question.

"She goes around helping Americans," said Tommy. "If one of them is robbed or gets into jail in a foreign country, she comes along and gets him out. The government keeps her for that."

"Let us hope," said the king, "that we'll never have to stand in front of her."

"I don't think," said Tommy apologetically, "that she would shoot at a king. I was just telling you—"

"Let us hope that she won't have to shoot at anybody for a long while to come. And now, you must promise me to stop dropping shooting-crackers on kings. It's dangerous— particularly to the kings."

Tommy arose.

"I'm sorry," he said, "if I scared you. I didn't mean it. I just wanted to have some fun. I—I hope you won't think hard of me."

The king grasped Tommy's hand.

"You're forgiven," he said. "You have our—that is, my pardon. And now you run along and tell your father not to let you carry shooting-crackers about Europe."

"He didn't know it," protested Tommy. "It wasn't his fault. He and my mother were out at dinner."

"Give them my compliments," said the king.

His majesty pressed a button, and a functionary appeared at the door.

"And if you care to see some fireworks," he continued, "bring your father and mother to the *Garten* tonight. I have been away and—well, when a king comes home, it's the custom for his people to make a holiday of the day, to show him that they are satisfied with the way he is ruling them. There'll be fireworks—"

Tommy was delighted.

"Just like at home!" he said.

"Yes," said the king. "I think you'll enjoy it. And, by the way—"

He stopped and scribbled something on a piece of paper—

"This will admit you and your father and mother to the palace," he said, "and you can look at the fireworks from one of the windows."

"Thank you, sir," said Tommy. "Thank you, sir!"

The king, in truth, was unusually nice, mighty nice—as nice as could be imagined.

"And now, be good," he said in farewell. "Your property will be returned to you. Goodbye!"

Tommy went back to the hotel in a carriage, with three soldiers on horseback riding at each side, and his head swam in recollection of his interview and in anticipation of the fireworks that night.

But he did not see the rockets, and he did not again see the king. Instead, he spent the evening *incommunicado,* in his room at the Rheinstadter Hof, meditating upon the burdens of life and the peculiar painfulness of parental slippers.

THE LAST CAVALRY CHARGE

AFTER MANY years, the gods that watch over cabbages and kings answered the War Lord's prayers by sending him a real war. It came unexpectedly, and, rather unfortunately for the War Lord's dreams of glory, it was with one of the nasty little powers without friends, and a larger and more spectacular conflict between two other nations was raging in another hemisphere at the time. But, despite these drawbacks, it was a real war, lawfully and regularly declared and begun, and so the War Lord was grateful and resolved to go to the front, to see what manner of entertainment it might furnish. Also, he had ideas—a good many of them—regarding the supply of ammunition in the field, the uselessness of cavalry, the efficacy of broad-pointed bayonets and other things, and there might arise opportunities to test them in practice. When these opportunities came, the War Lord wanted to be on hand.

The big war on the other side of the globe was being fought by engineer officers in overalls and a peculiarly tough breed of Mexican mules. There was little prancing of horses or waving of plumes in either army. The infantrymen lay in damp trenches as long as they could, and called down curses upon the Chicago meat packers, who sold to both sides with profitable impartiality, the preserved sinews of the ox, the sheep, and the swine. Only when the last parallel got so near the enemy's breastworks that the distance between might be covered in a hop, a skip, and a jump; only when the work of the engineers was so far accomplished did the gallant patriots in the trenches fare forth to shed their blood.

The War Lord, noting these things, resolved to make his own little war a model of all that modern warfare should be. So he dismounted his few remaining regiments of cavalry on the line, made a brigadier general of engineers commander of his right wing — to the violent scandal of the service — and brought an airship expert and ten airships from St. Louis, Missouri, at a cost of many thousands of dollars. With him, when he set off for the front, journeyed thirty-five gilded attachés, a personal staff of twenty-two sabres, sixteen apprentice war correspondents too tender to send to the real war across the world, and the First Royal and Imperial Regiment of King's Hussars, the melancholy remnant of the once-proud corps of mounted Life Guards.

The troopers of the Imperial, Etc. Regiment still rode horses and wore gauntlets, as they had at Minden and at Waterloo. But this was merely a sop to tradition and romance, and no one expected them to do more than group themselves artistically behind his majesty and carry messages where there were no field telephones or signalmen. Twenty years before, an obscure military critic in Belgium had sounded the knell of cavalry in a remarkable essay that brought him the red and green ribbon of the Order of the Crusaders from the War Lord, who was then serving his first year as king. Now, opinion was fairly unanimous. Cavalry could not charge machine guns.

And so the war was begun, and many battles were fought, all according to the most scientific principles, and, finally, there came a day when the consolidated forces of the nasty little Power were forced into a group of low hills and challenged to acknowledge defeat or prepare for annihilation. It had been a pretty conflict from the start, and a good many theories had been disproved and proved. The medical staff, for instance, had demonstrated beyond a doubt that foot-soldiers needed ten percent more protein a day than the world's experts had believed was necessary, and the airship man from St. Louis, before he was killed, had dropped a thousand pounds of a new Japanese explosive into the enemy's chief fortress and badly scared the soldiers in the bomb-proofs. Also, there had been obtained new data regarding the course of nickel-tipped bullets through sound tissue, and some interesting information as to the value of automobile wagon trains. All in all, it had been a mighty profitable and instructive war, and the War Lord rather regretted that it was so near its end.

It was eight miles, as the crow flies, along the enemy's front and the general in command, who was the engineer brigadier aforesaid, promoted and seasoned, decided that, for many reasons, it would be unwise to attempt a general flanking movement.

"As I look at it," he said to the War Lord in the privacy of his map- and wire-littered tent, "the easiest way to get through their front and turn them inside-out is to advance all along the line and feel out the weakest place. Then, when we find it, we can make a rush and follow it up by sweeping into them from both flanks and carrying them off their feet."

The general-in-command was suffering from a bad attack of sciatica and sat in a steamer chair, with his left leg propped upon a campstool. The fruit of a youthful visit to the United States to study bridge-building was a brownish, gummy corncob pipe. Each spring, he imported a dozen of such pipes, and whenever official etiquette did not demand that he wrestle with a cigar, he smoked one of them. Just at present, he was violating the laws of etiquette most outrageously by smoking at all, for it is not decent to puff acrid vapors into the face of a king, but the War Lord said nothing. In his majesty's private code of fundamental principles, it was set down that a general in command of an army, as the Creator's most striking masterpiece, could do no wrong. He, himself, was the general in command of the general-in-command. Sometimes, this particular general-in-command seemed to forget the consideration due royalty, and now and then his financier-like directness of manner and low emotional development rather irritated the War Lord. But, in the main, he remembered that the state archives and newspaper dispatches would say that his sovereign "commanded in person" and so it usually pleased him to be polite and affable. This flattered the War Lord and distracted his attention from his theories. It was something to be favored with the confidence of such a redoubtable soldier.

"Where do you expect to break through?" asked the War Lord, making a show of studying a map on the general's field table.

The general leaned very painfully and placed a dirty forefinger upon a wavy line denoting a stream descending through the hills.

"There," he said. "Miller-Bernhardt is below here," and the grimy forefinger moved a bit, "with Czermy's brigade and two regiments of Neuhaus', and the Seventeenth battery of field guns. He'll work his way up during the night and, at dawn or thereabout—"

A telephone signal buzzed insistently.

"There's Miller-Bernhardt now," said the general-in-command to the War Lord. And he directed himself to explaining the minor details to the division commander, who talked to him from the kitchen of a farmhouse six miles away. "Try to get into the mouth of the valley," he explained into the telephone's transmitter, "before they start down . . . and then, when you push in their screen, run for it and speed out . . . . The main thing is to keep them busy . . . . I wouldn't waste more than a regiment on those machine guns . . . . Try to reach them with your seven-pounders . . . .

No; don't risk a rush . . . yes, of course . . . . You'll have to pass them to westward . . . . And let me know as soon as you get under way."

So saying, the general-in-command sank back upon his chair and groaned dismally, for sciatica is not a pleasant malady, and he had many concerns upon his mind.

THAT EVENING, the War Lord dined with him in private, upon canned Smithfield ham from Chicago, vegetables of the countryside, and preserved peaches from California; and after dinner, he spent a few hours smoking his corncob pipe and reading the papers from home, which printed long attacks upon the cruelties of the censorship and bitter, leftist criticisms of the army, the war party, the War Lord, and himself.

At two o'clock, just as a faint booming from the westward confirmed the telephone's news that the battle was begun, the general had his orderly pull off his boots and stretched out for his night's repose. Nothing of much importance was likely to happen until daylight, and if there was need for him, the alert lieutenant at the switchboard would awaken him. Two staff colonels in the tent next door played keno gloomily by lamplight. A major-general and a dozen or more captains and majors directed the transmission of ammunition from a row of desk telephones in a hay-shed across the road. Now and then, a snorting automobile puffed along the moonlit country highway, bearing medical supplies or signalmen.

Just as the first breath of dawn-wind from the south spread balm upon the chill of the night—for it was late in August—the War Lord and his personal staff arose sleepily and moved off, with clatter of hoofs and rattle of sidearms, toward the west, where Miller-Bernhardt and his men were preparing for their dash into the enemy's center. It was here, the general-in-command had decided, that it would be most feasible to attempt the turning inside-out, and the War Lord wanted to be where there was the greatest strategy and maneuvering and slaughter.

As the little cavalcade cantered on, the birds sang in the trees as merrily as if war had died with Hannibal and the boom of field pieces ahead seemed faint and far away. At a little wayside village, the War Lord stopped a frightened rustic in charge of a milch cow and gave him a gold piece for an earthen pot of foaming milk. It would make a pretty incident for the newspapers and the histories. Further on, he reined his horses at the base of a hill to watch the Third Army Corps medical staff arrange a field hospital in a grove. The surgeon-colonel in charge of it had his eye upon the grand cross of the Order of St. Lazarus and greeted the War Lord effusively.

"May I offer your majesty a stirrup cup of champagne?" he asked, in his best levee manner, as the War Lord remounted.

"No," replied the War Lord, firmly—he was a soldier, this king—"but—ah—if you have such a thing as—a bottle of beer—"

And so, the officers of the staff drank a bottle of cold beer each and stoically resigned themselves to the loss of the champagne. It was another anecdote for the paragraphers and the pulpiteers.

Just as the gorgeous staff got under way again, there was a flash of red and a glimmer of steel over the crest of the hill behind, and the First Royal and Imperial Regiment of King's Hussars, 645 strong, came into view. Lieutenant-Colonel Oscar Ivanovitch aus dem Hohe, its commander, rode twenty paces in advance of the first-troop—a slight, concave-backed sandy-haired young man, with the blood of half the grand ducal families of five nations in his veins. Three hundred years before, another colonel of his race and name had led the First Hussars in a charge that changed the map of Europe. Since then, son had succeeded father, and grandson, son, and aus dem Hohe arms gleamed red and gold in the lower left-hand corner of the regiment's colors. Colonel aus dem Hohe the Twelfth was a young man and proud—for hadn't his ancestors refused three minor kingdoms?—and it sickened him, as a man is sickened by a noxious draught, to tag along in the wake of the gilded and useless barons and princes of the imperial staff—younger sons, ballroom warriors, five-bottle men, and ladykillers, all of them. Thrice, almost on his knees, he had petitioned the smoke-enshrouded general-in-command for an assignment worthy the regiment's history and his own stanbaum. But, each time, he had been ordered off to hold unimportant railroad crossings or to scout like an *opéra bouffe* field marshal in the army's rear, and each time he had left the presence disconsolate. Now he was commanded to follow the imperial staff and to report himself to General Miller-Bernhardt for "scout duty" and "to keep open the lines of communication."

The War Lord, seeing the regiment come over the crest of the hill, halted to admire it and permit it to overtake him. When the gloomy young colonel came up, he wheeled into line beside him and saluted pleasantly, as any king would salute a fellow man whose forbears had cast the deciding vote at a change of dynasty.

It grew warmer as the sun mounted higher and higher, and by the time the War Lord and the First Hussars reached General Miller-Bernhardt's headquarters, the advance ordered by the general-in-command was well under way. General Miller-Bernhardt had seen fit to modify his orders somewhat, and the result was a rather nasty situation. Instead of a brigade, he had sent forward a single regiment to begin the advance up the valley, between the hills. This regiment had got by the machine guns on the right-hand hill and the artillery on the other in safety, but, after that, it had suddenly vanished from sight behind a spur in the valley. Now, communication with it was lost and there was no telling whether it was consuming the enemy's center or was being itself consumed.

General Miller-Bernhardt, perspiring in his tent, seemed much excited when the War Lord entered, and if the truth must be told, the general-in-command, at the other end of the six miles of telephone wire, was also excited. He demanded to know why the lost regiment had been sent forward without proper supports, as provided in the regulations, and why, at the indecent hour of 8:30 o'clock, the enemy's front still stretched along its thunderous eight miles without a breach. General Miller-Bernhardt couldn't explain these things satisfactorily, and the general-in-command belabored him with heavy sarcasm.

"Neuhaus is with it," protested Miller-Bernhardt. "It's von Braun's regiment—the 68th. I'm sure it's all right—"

"But where is it?" demanded the general-in-command. "Didn't you send any signalmen with it?"

"I can hear the firing from—"

"But who's doing the firing? " yelled the commander-in-chief into the telephone. "Does Neuhaus think he's got a whole army corps? Hasn't he got any line of communications at all?"

"I expect—"

"Expect— Go after him and obey your orders. I want both of those hills by noon."

The hills mentioned by the general-in-command were those to either side of the narrow valley up which Neuhaus and the 68th had marched. Neuhaus advanced in the face of a heavy crossfire, and by a most remarkable series of dashes had got by the enemy's guns and blundered on up the valley. Maybe he thought that adequate supports were following him. Maybe he didn't care. Miller-Bernhardt had expected that the heavy guns on the left-hand hill would halt him, and had planned advances up both hills by other regiments. But Neuhaus had swept on in his amiable fashion, and now Miller-Bernhardt faced the necessity of making the attacks on the two hills, suddenly and desperately, to rescue him.

Thus it happened that he wrestled with more trouble than even a division commander could tackle with equanimity. Just as he was bawling fresh orders into the ears of the staff officers who stood by telephones and waiting horses, the War Lord rode up with his staff and Colonel aus dem Hohe. Miller-Bernhardt heartily wished them all in perdition.

"You look excited," observed the War Lord pleasantly as he parted the tent doors and stepped in. Tell a debutante that her hair is out of curl, or even an archbishop that his sermons are silly or an actor that he rants, but never, gentle reader — if fate ever drains you from your comfortable fireside and puts you down in an armed camp — never, if you value your life, tell a general of division that he seems excited.

"No, your majesty," replied Miller-Bernhardt heavily, "I beg leave to correct you. I am not excited; I am busy!" And the War Lord retired to a knoll whereon stood Colonel aus dem Hohe and the officers of the staff. It was not an anecdote for the histories.

Czermy had two miles to march under plunging, long-range fire before he could get within the shelter of the glacial boulders that sprawled in the mouth of the valley.

Miller-Bernhardt roared orders into the telephone and danced with impatience as he watched the slow progress of the column of men in the plain that stretched, map-like, below.

Suddenly, there arose a fresh spluttering up the valley and the lost regiment came into view. It was three and a half miles straightaway from Miller-Bernhardt's tent door, but the plain was low and he could see up the valley as one can see across a square and up a street. There, he observed the clouds of smoke that marked Neuhaus' position. Evidently, the regiment was having a hard time of it, and had failed utterly in its attempt to break the enemy's center single-handed. On the hill to the right, hostile machine guns spouted flame. Behind Miller-Bernhardt, the 17th battery of field artillery roared at that with its seven-pounders, but the man who had emplaced them knew their business, and the hail of shells did not stop their cackling.

In a few moments, there was in progress as pretty a battle as ever unrolled itself before the eyes of a War Lord. Neuhaus' advance guard—once his rear—had fought its way back to the mouth of the valley, and all that remained of it—through the glasses, it seemed to be less than a hundred men—tried a swift movement around the base of the hill opposite that upon which roared the machine gun. Boulders favored it and the cataract of lead seemed to leave it unscathed. Behind it was faintly discernible the smoke of Neuhaus' main guard, fighting its way along the bases of both hills. Far to the left, on the plain below, Czermy's men were advancing to meet and support the heroic advance. And over all shrieked the shells from the 17th battery to the rear, and now and then, a shell or two from the enemy's battery of heavy artillery on the hill opposite that crowned by the machine guns. But all but one of these heavy pieces seemed to be out of action. The 17th had put its mark upon them before Neuhaus began his luckless advance.

Colonel aus dem Hohe stood by the War Lord, a dozen yards from Miller-Bernhardt's tent door, and watched the fight. Perspiration stood out in drops upon his forehead and he was pale and excited. For the first time in three hundred years, a man of his name was standing idly by, at the head of his regiment, and watching other men fight for their country. Once, twice, thrice, he begged Miller-Bernhardt for an order to advance.

"Let me take that hill," he pleaded, pointing to the slope crowned by the clamorous machine guns. "I could get up on the right side and rush them before—"

Miller-Bernhardt, red-faced and care-worn, permitted himself to smile.

"This is a battle," he said, "not a massacre."

Colonel aus dem Hohe flushed at this, for the War Lord had overheard, and glared at Miller-Bernhardt.

"I am not joking," he said icily. "I ask again for permission to advance."

"What chance would your cavalry have against those machine guns?" demanded the immovable Miller-Bernhardt with a sort of superior disgust. "Do you think I'm crazy? Do you want to make me the laughing stock of Europe?" He straightened up with flashing eye. "Not a hundred of you men," he concluded thunderously, "would get halfway up the hill."

"That may be," replied aus dem Hohe quietly. "I am not asking for a guarantee of safe conduct. I merely desire a chance to make a diversion and help Neuhaus get out of his—"

"You venture to criticize!" roared Miller-Bernhardt. "You think I've made a mess of it? You want to help me out? I order you—"

"Why not let him try?" said the War Lord, turning toward the division commander. He had overheard most of what had been said and the theatricality of the thing had appealed to him. Besides, the situation seemed to offer a good chance to test a theory. What if aus dem Hohe took the hill? What if his troopers rode into and over the machine guns? What if cavalry were still a serviceable arm after all, despite the theorists and the critics and the experience of two decades? Suppose the First Hussars turned the trick? How the world would sit up! How the textbooks would be changed! Certainly, it was worth the risk.

"Why not let him try?" said the War Lord.

Miller-Bernhardt, impatient, exasperated and, if the truth must be told, rather rattled, threw up his hands despairingly.

"If your majesty cares to take the blame," he said, "I am merely a soldier."

The sarcasm did not move the War Lord.

"It will be time enough to fix the blame," he said grandly, "when the day is ended. I think it's worthwhile to try."

Miller-Bernhardt, in high dudgeon, cloistered himself in his tent and made angry protest, by telephone, to the commander-in-chief. Meanwhile—all of this, you must remembers, took but a few minutes—Colonel aus dem Hohe, a smile upon his smooth face, shouted a quick order, and the First Imperial and Royal Regiment of King's Hussars, 645 strong, cantered up from the glade wherein its horses had been tethered and rode out into the open, with plumes waving and steel shimmering in the morning sunlight. The War Lord, glasses in hand, saluted admiringly as the ranks of shining chargers passed him. Here, at last, was something that might make the world forget the big war on the other side of the globe, and fix its mind, for a space, upon the War Lord and his army.

If you have ever seen a regiment of cavalry gallop across a parade ground, with a line of girls under parasols gazing on admiringly, you will know with what splendor and spirit the First Royal and Imperial Regiment of King's Hussars cantered down the winding road and into the low ground that separated the War Lord and his field glasses from the green hill of the machine guns, three miles away. Every trooper had his eyes to the front; every back was curved like a bow; every plumed head was erect and immovable. The very horses seemed to feel the portentousness of the march. Not only was the First Regiment going into action, but Cavalry itself, with its three thousand years of glory, was on trial for its life.

It was five minutes before the enemy noticed the gorgeous line of horsemen, for the smoke lay thick upon the hill of the machine guns, and five minutes more before the purpose of the movement seemed to be understood. That Miller-Bernhardt, even in the light of his morning's blunder, had ordered his cavalry to charge the hill, did not occur to the men at the top of it until the first troop was fairly at the bottom. Certainly, it was ridiculous enough to make any self-respecting soldier rub his eyes. Arabs and Somalis might do such things—but Europeans? Cavalry against machine guns? As well say putty blowers against battleships or riffles against bags of sand. It was incredible, astounding, absurd, impossible!

Far behind, with his eyes glued to his field glasses, the War Lord was dancing about excitedly.

"Why don't they fire?" he exclaimed. "It's a trap! Miller! Miller!"

General Miller-Bernhardt had been standing behind him.

"There's plenty of time for firing," said the general grimly. "I suppose they want to waste as few bullets as possible."

Then the War Lord and the general, through glasses, saw an officer of the enemy's army stand upon a boulder and gaze down the slops on the advancing horsemen. Of course, the distance was so great that it was out of the question, but the War Lord would have made oath that he saw him smile. Aus dem Hohe and his men were advancing up the rounded foot of the hill, in open order, and their horses were trotting slowly and heavily, as a cart horse moves, for the ground was steep and rough. The officer by the machine guns turned his glasses upon them again and then he dropped behind his boulder.

All the while, a few of the guns had continued to squirt lead down the left side of the hill in the direction of Neuhaus' advance guard, which was dodging along under fairly good cover in the mouth of the valley.

Suddenly, these guns became silent and Neuhaus, far below, rallied and formed his men. At the same time, a party of gunners in the enemy's dark green uniform began to struggle with the guns and to swarm over them. They were turning them around, so that their muzzles pointed down the right front of the hill, toward the advancing ranks of aus dem Hohe's troopers.

The War Lord saw the young colonel himself, his saber unsheathed and his horse afoam, climbing, climbing, climbing. Behind him, horses strained and stumbled and sprang into brief gallops and jumped clumsily over ditch and stone. It was a rough and a steep hill. Near the top, the slope grew easier and when it was reached, there would come an order to gallop.

"They'll do it! They'll do it! They'll do it!"

The War Lord pranced as if beside himself with excitement.

"Do what, sire?" asked the pessimistic General Miller-Bernhardt.

"Take the guns!" replied the War Lord. "A dash, and they'll have them!"

General Miller-Bernhardt took a calm and deliberate look through his glasses with an air becoming a division commander.

"I have my doubts," he said judicially. "I doubt it."

The War Lord saw the first puff of thin, white smoke from the machine guns ten seconds before he heard the faint rattle. As the smoke arose and drifted off in hazy wisps, there came a sudden transformation and it seemed, through the glasses, that the First Regiment had suddenly become stalled in a marsh. Two horses broke from the mass and galloped downhill, with something heavy dragging after each of them. Then two more appeared as dancing specks upon the hillside, and two more, and three more, and a dozen more. After that, the smoke grew so dense that the War Lord saw nothing else. It was as if a curtain had been run down in a play. General Miller-Bernhardt, emerging from his tent, raised his glasses and looked intently and long. A staff captain came from his tent and touched his arm.

"Suregon-Captain Schmillus is at the telephone, sir," said the captain.

"What does he want?"

"He wants to know how many surgeons you'll need from Hospital No. 4."

"Not many," said the general thoughtfully. "Tell him to send twenty—or, say, twenty-five. Make it twenty-five."

"Twenty-five, sir," repeated the captain.

Then General Miller-Bernhardt swept his glasses toward the mouth of the valley and allowed himself the luxury of a smile. Neuhaus' advance guard, re-formed, rallied, and re-inforced by his guard, was advancing up the left side of the hill, to what was now the rear of the machine guns. Czermy and his brigade were plodding from left to right along the base of the hills. In twenty minutes, they would be at the mouth of the valley, too. Only the 17th battery, on the hill beside the general, was idle. Officers and men were standing upon rocks, caissons and guns, watching the clouds of fretful machine-gun smoke upon the hillside three miles away. Under and within that smoke was the First Royal and Imperial Regiment of King's Hussars. Maybe it was fighting the fight of its history. Maybe its fighting days were over.

For twenty minutes, the cloud of smoke rested upon the hillside and the faint rattle came from afar. The War Lord, nervous and impatient, strained his eyes and anathematized his glasses. The smoke was white, billowy, opaque. Hussars, machine guns and the hill were behind it. Only a dim sound, as of a heavy wagon crossing a bridge, told the story of the fight—only the rattle and smoke. The machine guns were still in action. Aus dem Hohe's men had yet to cut down the gunner and take the crest. And if they were to do it at all, they had to do it swiftly.

Meanwhile, Neuhaus had picked up frantic signals from Miller-Bernhardt and was struggling up the hill in the rear of the guns, and Czermy, coming around from the left, was pressing his brigade through a wheat field. Five minutes passed, and then ten, fifteen, and twenty. Neuhaus' men seemed to be crawling like snails. Czermy was a mired ox in his wheat field. The War Lord stamped and paced up and down. General Miller-Bernhardt was more calm. He saw the solution of his difficulties unroll before him.

All things have an end, even in war, and, by and by, Neuhaus' shattered veterans reached the crest of the hill and fought for a moment with two companies of the enemy's infantry—man to man, arm to arm, shoulder to shoulder, cheek to jowl. It was dirty work, but it was short and decisive. Back went the enemy, broken and crushed, and, quickly, Neuhaus himself, an old man with a gray beard, dripping perspiration and blood, led the way upon the machine guns. More hacking and sweating and gasping—and one gun after another became silent. Czermy's brigade was at the mouth of the valley, the enemy's front was broken, the machine guns were taken. Miller-Bernhardt, back in his tent, made his exultant report to the general-in-command. If a regiment could fight its way in and back, a brigade could break the line as one breaks a lath over one's knee.

And so the smoke lifted and the War Lord peered through his glasses, and when the air grew clear enough, he saw all that remained of the First Royal and Imperial Regiment of King's Hussars. As he gazed, the curious thought came to him that it looked like six hundred red and silver flies, stuck upon a huge sheet of green flypaper.

Fifty horses were struggling in one ditch and, directly in front of the machine guns—it seemed, from where he stood, to be but a few feet—there was a great heap that moved and squirmed. A riderless charger, apparently unhurt, trotted slowly across the skyline, and Neuhaus' men, in their khaki, could be just faintly discerned as they moved down the slope and dragged the wounded up to the place where their surgeons were laboring with their own luckless companions and the few survivors of the foemen who had manned the machine guns. It was not pleasant to walk upon that slope. A wounded soldier crouches in the mud and waits in silence for stretcher or the darkness, but a horse—

"They're wig-wagging for more surgeons," said the War Lord, who prided himself upon the fact that he could read the flags as well as most men read a newspaper.

General Miller-Bernhardt turned to a staff officer.

"Send ten ambulances and ten doctors," he said.

The heavy wagons went clattering down the road into the plain like coaches bearing a merry party to a picnic. After them went a burial party from the reserves, with the enlisted men told off for double fatigue as a punishment for minor regulation-smashing. They were sent to cut the bridles and trappings from the horses and to render an account of them to the quartermaster's department, which is charged with the care of such things. A couple of hours later, as the sun was sinking westward, the ambulances began to come back, each with its burden. Ten of them came trudging by; the wounded were not many.

In his tent, Miller-Bernhardt dined with the War Lord and their talk was of strategy. The general was in affable mood, for the day had ended better than it began, and so he sipped his red wine and harkened unto the king.

"Just think of it!" said the War Lord. "Everybody said it couldn't be done. And, yet, the First Hussars—" he stopped and corrected himself—"my First Hussars did it!"

"With considerable loss," suggested Miller-Bernhardt discreetly.

"Of course," admitted the War Lord. "With very considerable loss." He paused and stroked his long mustachios. "In fact," he resumed, "you may say that their losses amounted to practical annihilation. But the essential point was gained. They advanced in the face of machine-gun fire—and took the hill."

"With the aid of Neuhaus," suggested Miller-Bernhardt.

"True enough," said the argumentative War Lord. "But Neuhaus would have been pushed back down the hill if they hadn't engaged the guns."

Miller-Bernhardt refilled his glass.

"I rather fancy," he said, "that the world will never see another cavalry charge."

The War Lord's eyes sparkled.

"Then all the greater the glory!" he exclaimed. "All the greater the glory for you—and me!"

Miller-Bernhardt wondered what the newspaper correspondents would say of it, and what the Leftists would charge on the floor of chamber.

"If your majesty will permit a reminder," he said, "you will remember that the charge was ordered by you, and not by me. Therefore, whatever glory arises—"

"Say no more," replied the War Lord royally. "I shall not forget your wise counsel."

Then they walked out of the tent, upon a little terrace that ran beside the wagon road, and watched the heavy ambulances pass by on their second trips to Hospital No. 4. One stopped, that its horses might rest, and the War Lord stepped down to peer into it. A surgeon sat upon a camp-stool within, bending over a man upon the floor. The man was in his underclothes and muddy, bloody bandages wrapped him in all directions. He was Lieutenant Colonel

Oscar Ivanovitch aus dem Hohe. The surgeon reached for a lantern on the driver's footboard, that his patient might see his visitor.

"Colonel!" exclaimed the War Lord, aghast.

Aus dem Hohe raised his head—and then it dropped upon his arm, and great sobs shook him.

"My men!" he moaned. "My men! My men! My men!"

The War Lord motioned to the surgeon.

"Will he die?" he whispered.

The surgeon was a truthful man.

"I am afraid not, your majesty," he replied.

And the ambulance rattled off into the night, along the road that led to Hospital No. 4.

PUBLICATION HISTORY

"The Defeat of Alfonso" was written in 1900, but first appeared in print in *The Youth's Companion*, January 14, 1926.

"The Cook's Victory" originally appeared in *Short Stories,* August 1900.

"The Woman and the Girl" originally appeared in *Short Stories,* February 1901.

"The Crime of McSwane" originally appeared in *Frank Leslie's Popular Monthly*, July 1901.

"Like a Thief in the Night" originally appeared in *Short Stories*, August 1901.

"The Flight of the Victor" originally appeared in *Frank Leslie's Popular Monthly*, September 1901.

"The Point of the Story" originally appeared in *Frank Leslie's Popular Monthly*, September 1901.

"A Double Rebellion" originally appeared in *Short Stories*, January 1902.

"Hurra Lal, Peacemaker" originally appeared in *Short Stories,* May 1902.

"Firing and a Watering" originally appeared in *Short Stories,* August 1902.

"The Passing of a Profit" originally appeared in *Short Stories,* January 1903.

"The Heathen Rage" originally appeared in *The Criterion*, September 1904.

"The Fear of the Savage" originally appeared in *The Criterion*, November 1904.

"The Bend in the Tube" originally appeared in *The Red Book Magazine*, February 1905.

"The Star-Spangled Banner" originally appeared in *The Monthly Story Magazine*, September 1905.

"The King and Tommy Cripps" originally appeared in *The Red Book Magazine,* July 1906.

"The Last Cavalry Charge" originally appeared in *The Red Book Magazine,* August 1906.

About the Author

Henry Louis Mencken, 1880–1956, the "Sage of Baltimore," was one of the most influential American journalists and critics of the first half of the 20th century, renowned for his keen intellect, independent judgment, and acerbic wit. Mencken's books include *The Philosophy of Friedrich Nietzsche* (1907), *In Defense of Women* (1918), *The American Language* (1919), *Prejudices* (1919–1927), *Treatise on the Gods* (1930), *Treatise on Right and Wrong* (1934), and his memoirs *Happy Days, 1880–1892* (1940), *Newspaper Days, 1899–1906* (1941), and *Heathen Days, 1890–1936* (1943).

Milton Keynes UK
Ingram Content Group UK Ltd.
UKHW011825041023
429950UK00001B/96